THE HEART OF MERCY

GEORGIA PEACHES

TANYA EAVENSON

WHAT READERS ARE SAYING

"*To Gain a Mommy*, by Tanya Eavenson is a sweet novella-length Christian romance. The plot is straight-forward and plausible. The characters are well-developed, and Ms. Eavenson's writing style is smooth and enjoyable. For those who like romance with strong Christian underpinnings, this is a good pick!" ~Carolyn

"*To Gain a Mommy* is story of former sweethearts with a mountain of hurt between them. Helping them through their journey to try to get past the pain are two adorable children, a loveable dog, and a mom/grandmother who knows the importance of dealing with hurts now. Add in a beach setting, and, oh, did I mention chocolate? If you're a fan of watching God heal hearts and bring sweet forgiveness, you definitely don't want to miss this one. And I dare say, you'll love the rest of the series as well. Buy. This. Book! You'll be glad you did!" ~Marie

"I love reading everything by this author! She brings her stories to life and holds your attention. This story is sweet, romantic, heartfelt, uplifting, and challenging. The couple embark on a journey of healing, seeking God, and allowing Him to work in their lives. It's a great read. I highly recommend this book!" ~Kris

"An enjoyable novella with great multifaceted characters that are realistic and with whom the reader can empathize and fall in love with. A plot that is interesting, engaging, enjoyable and a great easy read. For a novella, the author was able to develop a full story that isn't lacking in any one area, has dropped underlying issue and minor storylines." ~AJK

"It was so nice to see that Patrick Reynolds gets his happily ever after. I felt so sorry for him in the book *To Gain a Mommy*. This story made me realize that God has plans for each of us and we just need to be open to them. If you are a pet owner or love pets you will laugh at how inept Patrick is with animals. Thank goodness he is not that way with children since he is a pediatrician. I also liked the second chance theme in this story which made the story even better. What a fun, heartfelt story of finding love when you might least expect to." ~Lori

"This is the first of Tanya's books that I have read. I will definitely be purchasing and reading more books by her. She has entwined a thriller with love & Christianity. It is definitely a great read! I highly recommend it."
~Charlotte

"Brice and Madi are likable, well-rounded characters working together in a dangerous situation. The suspense kept me turning pages as I became more invested in their safety and in their growing attraction for each other. I also enjoyed the brief glimpses of characters from the first two novellas in the series. I've enjoyed all three novellas in this series and look forward to reading more books by Tanya Eavenson." ~E.M.

"I loved this book! It was a great romance watching the relationship strengthen between the two characters and suspenseful as I did not know what would happen to her or if there would be danger! Great book and loved to read similar." ~Jay

The Heart of Mercy

Published by All Roads Publishing Copyright © 2020 by Tanya Eavenson

On file at the Library of Congress in Washington, DC.

Ebook ISBN 978-1-945981-07-4

Print ISBN 978-1-945981-08-1

Scripture quotations, whether quoted or paraphrased by the characters, are taken from the King James Version of the Bible.

Cover Design by V. McKevitt

 Created with Vellum

"*W*hat?" Mercy Cunningham's scrubbing pad stilled on the greasy dish in the sink. "Who's back?"

"You know who. *Him*." Felicity, a loyal soup kitchen volunteer turned friend, plopped another empty aluminum pan in the soapy water. "Hey, Demetris," she called over her shoulder. "You got another tray of grits ready?"

He didn't look up from flipping pancakes. "No, but we have hash browns. One tray left." He gestured at it with his spatula.

Felicity maneuvered her way to the counter and snatched up the potholder beside the steaming pan of hash browns. "Mercy, go talk to him." She rushed out of the kitchen, but not before giving Mercy a riled look.

Their community homeless population was growing, and all Felicity thought about was the silent stranger in their midst. Why was she so hung up on finding out more about this guy? They knew little about most of their clients, except for what was filled out on the client sheet. Their silent stranger had illegibly scribbled on only the top line—his name, Mercy assumed. She was required to have paperwork on each person who visited the soup kitchen, but mostly she needed the numbers of people she fed each quarter. To Mercy, his mark was good enough. Financial funding kept the place alive—as well as most everyone who came through it, the way she saw it. An *X* or a scribble, she'd take it.

She plunged her hands back into the tub of hot, food-speckled water and continued loading the dishwasher. Her dad—president of a Fortune 500 company—continually tried to persuade her to use her degree to build a life and career that "mattered," but what really mattered to Mercy was helping people. At thirty-two, this was the life she wanted.

Finished loading the second set of dishes, Mercy pushed her dark hair from her eyes and washed her hands.

"Mercy." Tucker poked his head into the kitchen. "Someone's here to see you. He looks like a lawyer. Do you want me to send him away?"

She smiled. Tucker, who was working toward his undergraduate degree in social work, came in handy around here, but what he saw on a person's outside didn't determine what was on the inside. Everyone who stepped through their doors was either a father, a mother, a son, or a daughter to someone. They were important in the eyes of their Creator, regardless of what they looked like. "Tell him he'll need to wait another"—she glanced at the clock on the wall—"twenty minutes. Or he can make an appointment."

Tucker winked and disappeared.

She shook her head. He was such a flirt, but the kid had a heart of gold. "Demetris, how are we doing on food? They love it when we serve breakfast for lunch."

"We have a pan of biscuits and one pan of pancakes that I'm almost finished with. Everything else is out there."

"I think we'll have enough, though some will be eating nothing but starch. When I go to the food bank tomorrow, I'll see if they have extra meats for this week's menu. Is there anything else you can think of we might need?"

"Mercy?"

She turned at hearing Tucker's voice again. He stood just inside the doorway, his face pale.

Her heart dropped. "Is everything all right?"

"Well, that lawyer man, he says he'll see you now. He wouldn't take no for an answer. And when I mentioned making an appointment, he mumbled something under his breath that I'm sure I didn't want to hear."

She exhaled. "Six-one? Black hair? Gray around the temples?"

"Scary dark eyes? Uh, yeah. How'd you know?"

Eyes sliding shut, she just shook her head. *Dad. Why do you have to intimidate my volunteers? I can't lose another.*

Demetris chuckled, adding more pans to the murky water to be washed. "Her father can be ... persuasive."

"Father?" Tucker's voice rose an octave. "He's your father? Are you kidding me?"

The disbelief was nothing new. She and her father couldn't be more different. Mom had called him a surly bear and her a gentle dove. After her mom's passing, the differences between her and her father seemed to pull them apart. Mercy now had no one to stand in her corner for what she felt the Lord had called her to do—even if the opposition was her own father. "Tucker, please tell my dad I'll be out in a few minutes."

She went to her office and grabbed her airport carry-on bag from under her desk. Her emergency pack, she called it, for his unexpected visits. After withdrawing her brush, she released her half-fallen hair from its ponytail.

She glanced in the mirror—the one she'd hung in her office for just this occasion—and frowned. *What a mess.* And she probably smelled like greasy potatoes. Cooking with Demetris for three hours tended to do that. Nothing could be done about it, but she wouldn't change a thing. The food she smelled like was the only meal many people were getting today.

She brushed out the tangles, then stuffed her bag back under the desk and left her office. With a nerve-calming breath, she pushed through the kitchen doors to the serving stations and into the dining area. Her gaze found him right away. Immaculately dressed in his Armani suit, he stood surrounded by unwashed bodies in tattered clothes. She held her head high despite his disapproving look.

"Hi, Dad. Would you like to go into my office?"

"No. I'm fine right here." He pursed his lips, unblinking.

"I'm surprised to see you. You know you could have called."

"Mercy." His voice rose slightly. "We agreed to brunch last week. For ten this morning. That was an hour ago. You never showed. I was worried. What would you expect me to do?"

Her stomach sank. "Dad, I'm so sorry. I forgot."

"Obviously."

A few moments ticked by before she noticed they were the center of attention. When she asked to walk him to his car, he accepted with a short nod, so perhaps he'd noticed as well.

As soon as the door closed behind them, she apologized again. "I'll make it up to you."

"By leaving this place and working for me?"

They slowed at the driver's side door of his Bentley, and she met his dark gaze. Eyes so much like her own. "You know I can't do that."

"I don't understand why not. Have you looked around the neighborhood lately? Watched the news? This place isn't safe. What you're doing isn't safe."

How many times had they had this discussion? "But it's what I'm called to do."

"No, you're not called to risk your life day in and day out, and for what? People who care little to nothing about you. I love you and want you to be safe."

"I know you do, Dad." And he was right. When she'd read the newspaper and learned her beloved neighborhood now suffered opioid addition and unspeakable crimes, it had driven her to make the hard choice to serve only lunch and then close the doors shortly afterward. Yet the facility she'd opened last year, two blocks from the soup kitchen, housed fifteen homeless residents, men and women alike, from the community. "I know it's hard, but the Lord is making a difference here, and He's using me in the process. Two of my residents at The Lighthouse, for the first time in years, are holding jobs. In this program, they're being given a second chance at life."

"I never said you weren't doing a good thing. You can oversee projects similar to these, but in a safer environment."

She glanced at the building. "But if I wasn't here … what would happen to these people? We both know the alternative. I can't do that, let fear run me off. Well, I could, but I won't."

"You're so stubborn."

She grinned. Who did he think she'd inherited that streak from? They were so different and yet so much alike in some ways.

"What's so funny?"

She reached out and took his hand, though he rarely showed affection. "I'm sorry I missed brunch with you. That's on me. I had to let one of my cooks go, so I helped Demetris with the cooking. I am sorry. Can we reschedule?"

He gave her hand a squeeze before pulling away to search his pockets. "I'll have my secretary call you." He unlocked his car and opened the door, then paused to face her. "I've yet to see your new place."

"I know."

He nodded and slid in, making his point clear.

But how could she tell him her new apartment never

happened? Instead, she'd moved in with fifteen homeless residents, with one more on the way.

Mercy waved as her father drove off. She needed to come up with a plan and fast.

~

Noah Allen was a wanderer, and that was what he'd scribbled on the form he'd been required to fill out last year when he found himself hungry. What were a few measly words offered in exchange for a hot meal?

Between those days and this one had been a long side trip to Tennessee. While away, he'd had the nagging feeling he should never have left, and last week, something began pulling him back. Even against his inner alarm system. It blared this city's easy accessibility to pills could be a problem.

The caution was potent, real. But that tug to come back...

He no longer believed in the idea of the Lord leading someone to a certain place or being given a particular purpose in life. So why was he here, back in Atlanta, and at what cost? The only thing he had left in this world was his sobriety. Would he lose that too?

Noah entered the soup kitchen, and the aroma knocked him in the gut. He hadn't realized how hungry he was or how weak his legs were until his last steps to the food line. It had been two days since he'd eaten a regular meal, and though dumpster diving pulled him through, it seemed longer now since he'd had more than scraps.

With shaking hands, he shifted his backpack, the

weight of his only possession pulling him closer to the ground. Lightheadedness tried to overtake him, but he fought it off. He'd dealt with this before. It was getting worse, but if the shakes from withdrawal hadn't taken him, a little blood sugar trouble sure wouldn't.

He took a step forward in the line and collected a foam tray from the stack, not meeting the gaze of the boy who held out a loaded scoop of potatoes.

"Hash browns?"

He nodded.

"Glad you came back."

That made Noah drag his sluggish gaze up from his tray. A moment later, the swinging door from the kitchen opened and he saw her. Mercy, they called her. Whether that was her real name or not, it fit. She attended to the people who came in. Speaking to each one as if they were long-lost friends. Giving them blankets, pillows, and water. Feeding them.

As the door closed, he looked away, stepped to the next server, then made his way to two more, still aware of the tremors in his hands. Plate full, he found a spot on the floor near the entrance just as a man dressed in a tailored suit stalked inside and demanded to speak with Mercy.

Noah's fork slowed on its way to his mouth as he scanned the room. Many others were aware of the man's presence, but no one made a move except for the boy serving.

"Can I help you, sir?"

"Yes. Tell Mercy someone's here to see her."

He nodded and disappeared into the kitchen, only to

come back moments later. "She'll be out in twenty minutes, or if you'd like, you can make an appointment."

"Tell her I will see her now."

The boy froze and then returned to the kitchen.

The man glanced at his gold watch, then clasped his hands behind his back.

Mercy soon emerged from the kitchen with an expression Noah could only call stoic. It made him smile.

"Hi, Dad," she said. "Would you like to go into my office?"

Dad? This man was her father? Noah glanced between them. That couldn't be. They looked nothing alike. And the way they were dressed ...

Her father's voice rose, catching Noah's attention. "We agreed to brunch last week. For ten this morning. That was an hour ago. You never showed. I was worried. What would you expect me to do?"

"Dad, I'm so sorry. I forgot."

"Obviously."

The energy and tension in the room were thick, and all eyes were on them. They must have sensed it because in the next breath, they were walking outside.

Noah took a bite and inwardly moaned. The warmth of the hash browns, the taste ...

Suddenly the room seemed to sway. So hot. His heart pounded. He pressed a hand against his chest, swallowed the bite, and opened his mouth to call out for help.

Everything went black.

CHAPTER 2

*M*ercy rushed into the dining area.

Felicity paced back and forth, talking on her phone, while Tucker knelt beside their silent stranger, trying to rouse him.

"Yes, he's breathing," Felicity said into her cell and headed toward the kitchen.

"What happened?" Mercy dropped to her knees and hovered over the bearded man, who looked more like a duck hunter than a man who'd weathered life on the streets.

Tucker shrugged a shoulder. "Someone said he was drunk and passed out, but he didn't seem drunk a few minutes ago. He doesn't smell of alcohol."

"Help me get his jacket off. He probably passed out from heat exhaustion. It's ninety degrees, and he's wearing a jacket with a Sherpa lining." She began unbuttoning the clasps.

The last button and zipper were undone by the time

Felicity returned with a wet rag, which she handed to Mercy. "The ambulance is on its way."

Mercy dabbed his brow. "Hey, can you hear me? Will you wake up for us?"

At his lack of response, she continued to his cheek with the wet cloth. Funny. He didn't smell of sweat and urine but of spice and lemon. The man had taken a bath not long ago. "I wish I knew your name." She moved his shoulder-length hair to the side, then ran the cloth across his neck.

His long lashes fluttered, and he moved his head slightly.

"I think he's coming to," Tucker said.

An ambulance siren sounded in the distance.

"I'll meet them outside." Felicity headed for the door.

"Will you wake up? I can't have someone passing out on my watch."

His eyes opened slowly, revealing gray irises. They tracked erratically, but his breathing was steady. He blinked several times, then grimaced.

"Take it easy. Close your eyes for a few moments."

He did, and when he opened them again, he looked more coherent.

"You're back." She grinned, relief washing over her. "How do you feel?" She ran the cloth along his jaw and neck. "Better?" When he didn't answer but continued to pierce her with his gaze, she started folding the rag so she could look away from him. "Do you know where you are?"

Outside, the sirens stopped.

No answer.

"You're in good hands now. The paramedics are here."

Felicity led the paramedics, who carried black bags, to where their silent stranger lay.

"How's he doing, Mercy?" Tim asked a few strides out, eyes on his patient.

She stood and moved out of the way. "He seems to be coming out of it."

Tim squatted beside the man and spoke softly to him while clipping an oxygen sensor to his finger. He then checked his blood sugar. "Fifty."

Mercy gasped. No wonder he was on the floor. "We have juice."

Brad, the other paramedic and one she wasn't as happy to see as she once had been, took out a handheld computer and typed. "Sir, would you like to take some oral glucose or would you prefer juice?"

"A drink."

"Felicity," Mercy said, "would you mind getting some apple juice for him?"

"Sure." She hurried into the kitchen.

As the medics explained to the man who they were and why they were there, Mercy stepped back to watch.

Demetris came to her side. "How is he?"

"He'll be okay. I think."

"You're not sure?"

"He's homeless and on the ground with low blood sugar." *Maybe if I'd noticed him as I walked out with my father, I could have helped.* "How okay can you be?"

"Point taken." Demetris nodded at them. "I wonder what Tim's saying."

"Must be important. I guess we'll soon find out."

As Tucker neared them, Felicity crisscrossed his path carrying a glass of apple juice.

"They want to take him to the hospital for an evaluation." Tucker plunged his shaky fingers through his hair. "He says he doesn't want to go."

Demetris placed his hand on Mercy's shoulder. "Go talk that man into going to the hospital. I think he needs a push, and you're just the woman to do it."

"I don't know about that, but I can try." She peered at Tucker as she passed him on the way to the silent stranger. This must have been Tucker's first experience with an emergency, and in his career choice, this wouldn't be his last.

The man's head was bowed when she reached him. In his hand was the glass of apple juice, which he unsteadily lifted to his lips.

"Well, gentlemen," Mercy said as she neared. "I hear your patient isn't interested in getting checked out at the hospital."

Tim shrugged. "He needs to get his sugar up or he'll end up passing out again."

Mercy crouched beside him. "What's your name?"

"Noah." His voice cracked.

"Hi, Noah. How are you feeling?"

He downed the rest of the juice. "I'm good."

"But if you go to the hospital, you'll know everything is fine. You'll be back here in a few hours."

"I'm not interested." He turned and met her gaze. Those gray eyes once again pierced her, searching.

She could sense his interest—in what, she wasn't

sure. Her own interest brought unanswered questions. Why didn't he want to go to the hospital? Had something happened in his past to cause him to refuse treatment?

A few minutes later, Tim took Noah's blood sugar again. "One hundred ten."

Brad closed his laptop and stuffed it back into his bag. "Mercy, it would be best if he got checked out."

"I'm not going." Noah frowned and started to get up, but he was too unstable to stand and lowered himself back to the floor.

"I rest my case," Brad said.

Mercy looked from him to Tim. "Can I talk to you both for a minute?" She led them over to Demetris, so he would be included in their conversation. Hopefully, they were out of Noah's earshot. Tucker stayed with him, and Felicity started encouraging the people remaining in the dining area to leave. They were fifteen minutes late closing already, and the free entertainment was over. She hoped.

"I'll take him in," she said, although unsure why she offered even as the words left her mouth. "I have a spare room at The Lighthouse, and he's more than welcome to have it. I can keep an eye on him."

"Mercy, he doesn't need a nurse," Tim said. "He needs a cook."

"Well, I have one. And leftovers from lunch anytime he wants to eat. Besides, your wife is heading to my place tonight to check on Wilma."

"This one is up to Brad. But I'm fine leaving Noah in your care as long as my wife checks him out when she sees

Wilma." Tim strolled back to his equipment and began packing up.

"Mercy ..." Brad began, exasperated.

She knew what he was going to say. This wasn't their first time having this conversation. "Aren't we supposed to take care of the needy, the less fortunate ones around us?"

"He isn't your responsibility."

"Then whose is he? Just because someone made a bad choice doesn't mean you can just sit and watch them drown."

"*Choices.* You don't become homeless by making one bad decision. And I know this is hard to hear, but sometimes they don't want to be helped."

"But sometimes they do. They only want someone to take a chance on them."

"If only you could have extended that grace to me." Brad looked to his feet and took a heavy breath.

Demetris slipped into the kitchen, leaving them alone.

It was true. If only she could have extended Brad that same grace. Back then, he'd been engaged to be married to someone else and had never said a word. They'd only been seeing each other for a few months, but the calls at night, opening her heart as she'd never done before ... It'd crushed her. More than he would ever know.

Brad looked toward the kitchen. "Demetris, you'll cook for him?"

"Of course," he called back.

Brad turned back to her, and what she saw in his gaze reminded her of a doused fire. "Mercy, listen—"

"He'll be fine."

Shoulders slumped, Brad walked off.

Demetris' eyes narrowed as he walked back to her. "I didn't know he still had feelings."

"He shouldn't. All that's in the past."

"I'm not sure he agrees. He never married."

Her gaze shifted to Brad and the move of his tight lips as he spoke to Noah. *What might have been*, her heart whispered. She gave Demetris a sad smile. "But I did get married. To this place and to the homeless of Atlanta."

CHAPTER 3

*M*ercy snuck a sideways peek at Noah's scraggily profile as they walked two blocks to the house. *What am I doing?* She knew nothing about this man.

She wanted to scold herself for going against every procedure she'd ever written, procedures that safeguarded her and the others in the house. There was a process for this: an application, phone calls with references, face-to-face interview, as the applicants were vetted.

How was she going to handle things now? Give him a crash course on how things were done? She hadn't written a manual for this deviation from script.

It hit her all at once as she reached the house, there'd been no commitment made on his part, only hers. But the facility didn't work that way. It was meant to be an equal partnership.

She paused at the door and faced him. "Noah, I know I said you were welcome here, and you are, but I've never invited anyone to stay at the house I haven't vetted and prayed over beforehand. There's a lot that needs to be discussed. After I go over these things, you are free to stay or to go, but it's something we need to talk about today."

"I understand," he said shortly.

"And that includes paperwork that must be legible, filled out completely, including some questions that might be difficult. But they must be filled out. Agreed?"

He nodded.

She accepted the non-verbal agreement and opened the door. "Welcome to The Lighthouse." Emotion caught in her throat as it always did when she brought someone new to the house, the house God gave her to help others. It still amazed her, and thankfulness filled her heart. "I do hope you'll enjoy your time here. I'll take you to your room, but first, here's the living room to your right. Kitchen and dining room to your left. My office is off from the kitchen."

Noah followed her down the hall.

She slowed in front of his room but pointed at the next corridor. "There is one shared bathroom at the end of each hallway. You'll find one more in the dining area. And this door right here leads to your room."

As she unlocked the door and stepped aside for him to enter, she didn't mention that her room was next to his. There wasn't much in his room, a twin bed and a wooden dresser she'd found at a secondhand store, but if he stayed, it would be his home.

"I'll let you get settled in but not for long. Susan, she's a doctor who makes house calls, should be here in two hours, and we have paperwork to do before then. Meet me in the kitchen in about twenty minutes. We can grab a snack before we talk. Sound good?"

He nodded again and slipped his backpack from his shoulder. "Thank you."

Mercy smiled and left him to unpack.

She went to her office, grabbed a packet of paperwork, and found Demetris already in the kitchen making a list for the week's menu. He was also The Lighthouse cook, and she was grateful. If she were the one preparing meals for everyone, they'd be better off on the streets. Growing up with a chef should have granted her a few skills, but when she'd ventured out on her own, she'd quickly realized how wrong she'd been not to learn how to cook.

"How's it goin' with Noah?"

She set the packet down and leaned over his list, catching a glimpse of what their meals would be. "We'll see. We're to meet here in a little bit. It will give us time to talk and fill out paperwork before Susan arrives."

"He's agreed?"

She shrugged and moved to the fridge. "Said he would, but we know how that goes. Sometimes laziness holds people back, or a past that's too much for a person to handle."

"What's your gut sayin' about 'im?"

She laughed at that as she collected two bottled waters. "And you think that's how I make decisions?" She set them on the counter.

"You accepted me, didn't you? With a gut instinct and

a prayer." He smiled and jotted another item on the notepad.

Demetris, a hulk of a man, not tall, but in width and strength, had been a bouncer in his old life, while nursing dreams of attending culinary school. In the new, he'd taken on the role of protector and big brother. At first, she hadn't been sure what to think, especially since she had seven years on his twenty-five. After the interview, she'd seen that this job would give him purpose, and she couldn't deny him that. Besides, she always wanted a big brother. She loved how God was in the details and provided her with a hand of protection and blessed her with a dear friend.

She shook her head as she gathered snack items. "Got me there. But look at where you are now. You're one of God's success stories. What a testimony."

Demetris stopped his writing and pointed his pencil at her. "I've got you to thank. Without you ..."

"Without each other. We're a team. I couldn't do this, cook for everyone, day in and day out. You know I burn things."

He went back to writing, but she caught the lift of his mouth. He knew he was needed, by her and everyone in the house. Accountability was something she tried to instill in everyone who stayed. One of those ways was through chores. Without each other's help, the house ran poorly, and every job was important. Teamwork was crucial, even if one of her newer residents didn't think so.

"What you got there?" Demetris came to stand beside her. "I can fix you something besides peanut butter and crackers."

"Oh, this isn't for me but for Noah. I'm fine."

A dark brow rose.

Believability was the key here, but she was fine. Kinda. Her stomach had only growled a couple of times.

"I noticed you didn't eat this morning. Matter of fact, I can't remember the last time you ate breakfast. Are you trying to starve your hips to a size of negative three?"

"Hardly, but you're right. I should eat."

Without another word, Demetris dropped his pencil and took a dish from the fridge. "I saved you a plate. Breakfast."

Noah strolled into the kitchen, his gaze taking in the room and Demetris, then stopping at her. Their eyes held for a moment longer before he looked away. She couldn't help being aware of him. Even with his unkempt hair and massive beard, his gray eyes, the palest she'd ever seen, were oddly beautiful. But it was the unexpressed sadness she found there that drew her. Different from others in that anger was missing. Yet, there was something else within those crystal orbs … something so deep she'd caught only a glimpse of it the first time she'd seen him. It hadn't made an appearance since. A loneliness perhaps, an abandonment she couldn't begin to comprehend.

"Hi," she said as she carried the plate of crackers to a nearby table. "We can sit here. These are for you. Let me grab the packet from the counter, and we can get started." She headed to where the microwave ticked away the seconds, and Demetris continued with his list.

She snatched up the bulging blue folder, returned to the table, and slid the folder across the table to Noah. "There's a new pen inside. You're welcome to keep it."

Demetris strolled to her with a plate in hand, giving her an accusing glance. "This woman here doesn't eat enough to keep a cricket alive. I have to keep her straight." He set the plate in front of her.

"It's true, Noah. He keeps me fed. I'd shrivel up without him, and he knows it." She lifted her fork and pointed to Demetris. "Noah, this is Demetris. He's our cook extraordinaire." Stabbing an egg with her fork, she took a bite and moaned. "My point exactly."

"My work here is done. Nice to meet you, Noah." A moment later, Demetris stepped out.

Noah nodded before his gaze fell to the folder. He reached over and flipped the cover open and pulled it toward him.

As she ate, she couldn't help but notice his hands as he filled out sheet after sheet. They weren't worn and cracked, but clean and smooth, like that of a man who did office work, like her father. His nails weren't long or broken. Just the opposite, they were neatly trimmed and didn't hold much dirt. She was tempted to ask what he was doing here, sitting at a table with her, in this part of town, but took another bite instead. She'd find out soon enough once the paperwork was complete. Everyone who transitioned to the house joined the work force, and Noah would be no different if he planned to stay.

"Don't forget about the crackers. You can't let them go to waste."

He grabbed one, his focus never leaving the paperwork, and stuffed it in his mouth.

She ate her last bite and looked at Demetris as he re-entered the kitchen and went back to his notepad.

Noah paused and glanced at her, then slid a filled-out form onto the completed pile and started another.

"Do you mind if I look through these to get started?"

His eyes narrowed, and the tips of his fingers turned white from their pressure on the pen, but he nodded, remaining focused.

She was tempted to glance over the sheet he was working on but thought better of it. Instead, she gathered the completed forms, which the man had kept in order. It was the first time a client had ever done so, and he intrigued her that much more.

Mercy flipped the pack over and found their silent stranger's information.

Full name: Noah Peter Allen

Age: 38

What jobs have you held? Garbage collector. Painter. Construction. Plummer. Bus driver.

A lock of hair slid across her gaze, and she tucked her hair behind her ear and continued to read through the pages, taken in by his answers. She couldn't reconcile them with the man sitting with her. She paused and glanced up to find him observing her. "Is there something on your mind?"

His eyes darted away.

"If you have a question …?"

Those gray eyes returned to her and held. "How did you end up at the shelter? Your father, he was wearing Armani. He didn't seem pleased to find you here."

She raised a brow. *Father. Pleased. How would he even know what an Armani suit looked like?* "I could ask you the same question." She looked down at the paperwork. "Noah Peter Allen."

"Everyone calls me Noah."

She continued to read, seeing he had indicated no family or relatives to call in case of an emergency. No beneficiary. "Do you have anyone you can list in case of an emergency?" When he didn't answer, she looked to him.

His jaw clenched. "There's no one."

Mercy found it hard to believe that at such an age he had no one. She collected the pen and made a notation N/A on the line. Whether he was telling the truth, she'd find out, but for now, there was no need to push.

She skimmed the other papers and came to a form requesting to know his likes and dislikes, hobbies, and accomplishments. His handwriting had changed from clean cursive to tight, small loops, almost illegible. This was the form he'd struggled with. But why? This sheet wasn't required or prying, but one she asked for to become better acquainted with her residents and to help her know how to reward them for jobs well done.

Mercy pointed to one of the hobbies they shared. "You enjoy reading?"

"I think it might be best for both of us to just cut to the chase. The items listed were hobbies that once belonged to a man who's now dead."

She paused at his words, trying to think of what to say next. "Then who are you, Noah?"

"A skeleton of a man, waiting, yearning for another life."

"It's my hope and prayer that you'll find that here. Everyone needs a second chance at life."

"Everyone, or only those who want another try?" His voice lowered, and her heart ached at how hurt this man seemed. "It wasn't for the ones who were left to suffer in loneliness and memories."

"Noah, I can promise you, you aren't alone. And I know there's hope. I've seen it with my own eyes."

"In this place?"

"Yes. Hope is all around us, but sometimes we need to open our hearts so our eyes can see it. Sometimes, it's right in front of us. As small as a mustard seed."

"Like faith."

She eyed him. "Well, yes."

"Then let me be the first to tell you, a mustard seed of faith isn't enough. If it were, I could have healed the sick and raised the dead. And yet, the mountains did move. As they fell, they crushed me under their weight and almost killed me. How I wish they had."

Mercy was staring. She knew it. Never had someone during an interview process admitted to wishing they were dead. Whether he believed it or not, he was here for a reason, and with the Lord's help, he'd realize it too. "I'm glad you're not, but from what you've admitted, tomorrow you'll need to have a psychological evaluation to stay on, and when that's clear, we'll get you employed. Will that work for you?"

When he leaned back in his chair and nodded, she sensed the separation he put between them was more than space. Maybe to play her like others had, but she didn't feel it had been a lie, but truth, and for some odd reason he let her in. Either way, a psych eval was needed in this instance, and it forced her not to lead with her heart, but with her mind, and protect those in the house.

She forced her gaze to her paperwork, and with a quick prayer about how to proceed, she flipped to the last sheet and checked off two boxes.

"Hey, Demetris," Susan said, strolling into the kitchen. "Whatcha makin' for dinner? I'm starved."

"Beef stroganoff. Tell that husband of yours I can give him a few tips." He flashed her a wink.

Susan chuckled. "If a grill or smoker isn't included, he won't touch it with a ten-foot pole. But a girl can dream."

"Hey, Susan." Mercy collected her paperwork and stuffed it back into the folder. "Did Tim call you?"

"He did. Told me the situation. But someone's not too happy about it."

"He'll get over it. Let me introduce you to Noah. Noah, this is—"

"I heard. Susan." Noah looked to his hands.

"Then you've been introduced. Do either of you need anything from me?"

Noah shook his head.

Susan unlooped her stethoscope from her neck. "I think we're good. After I finish with Wilma, I'll find you and let you know how things went. If I need anything else, Demetris can help." She looked over her shoulder. "Isn't that right?"

"Always."

Mercy excused herself and walked back to her room with Noah's folder in her hand. She replayed their conversation, the heaviness of his words, and how emotions, feelings, or … something seemed to be communicating between them.

As she combed through his file, there was one thing she was sure of, he wasn't what he appeared to be.

CHAPTER 4

*N*oah set the rocking chair in motion, enjoying the solitude of the small area outside the shelter, even if the city noise joined him there. He'd learned quickly that no one visited the back porch except for a few birds. He used to spend hours in a hammock and still did when he went home.

The birds carried beautiful notes into the air, and if he closed his eyes, he could envision himself waiting for Bella to climb into their hammock beside him. She'd fall asleep in his arms, her blonde hair against his face. How he missed his wife.

His son.

He swallowed hard against the memories.

"Am I interrupting?" Mercy's gentle voice sounded next to him.

Fighting back the emotion, he drew his eyes tighter. *Yes.* He wanted to say. Instead, he opened his eyes and said nothing.

"Then I take it I am." The admission didn't stop her

from sitting in the rocker next to him and setting it in motion.

Noah waited for her to speak, to ask a question. Something. But she never said a word, just continued to rock.

He set his chair back into motion, listening not only to the noises around him but to the wood of the rockers pressing against the concrete as they moved back and forth. At first, their chairs sounded off-sequence, but after a few minutes, they rocked at the same rhythm in perfect unison.

Had she noticed? Done it on purpose?

Noah glanced at Mercy, expecting to see her smiling, but her eyes were closed. There was such a calming presence around her. He couldn't help but watch her as they rocked. He could see it in the upward tilt of her mouth, the relaxed nature of her shoulders, the folding of her hands in her lap.

Serenity. Peace. He found it next to her, even in the midst of the city's dissonance. The same peace he'd been chasing the last several years. He'd seen it in her over the few days he'd been a resident. It was evident when she helped a woman named Shameka find a job, or when Shameka's temper raged because alcohol wasn't allowed or because her room was too small. Or when another resident's son went to prison, Mercy helped the woman write a letter and send it in the mail. Mercy was strong but kind. And now she was with him, saying nothing, and yet her presence spoke volumes.

He closed his eyes and peace once again settled within his chest. The heaviness of life and death he couldn't shake seemed to slip away into the afternoon sun.

After a while, the rocker next to him slowed to a stop. He was tempted to look at her, but he kept his eyes closed.

Her light footfalls carried off into the distance and faded.

Who was this Mercy? And why when she left, did his peace fade with her?

Mercy entered the house, her mind on the man she'd just left. She always had to be willing to protect herself or defend others, whichever was needed, but the quietness between her and Noah was soothing and comfortable. She wasn't sure she'd ever felt such ease in the presence of one of her residents, or at all. Especially when everything about him was a mystery, and his pain seemed to be his curse.

She found Demetris in the kitchen preparing dinner. "Do you need any help?"

He turned to her with watery eyes. "I thought you'd never come." He exaggerated a sniffle.

She chuckled. "Give me the onions. Why do you insist on red onions? They are the worst. Buy Vidalia."

"The color makes the salad more interesting, and yet the favor tastes like a yellow onion. They're perfect."

"Thank you, Chef D, for that tidbit."

"At your service. Anything else you'd like to know?" He pointed to the tomatoes. "Mind cutting those?"

Mercy washed her hands and put on gloves. A knife

waited for her on the cutting board. He was always prepared. "What do you think about our new tenants, Shameka and Noah?"

"Honestly, Mercy. Shameka has a lot to work through, and I don't know if she can do that here. Her life is right out these doors and too convenient to get sucked back into. Noah, on the other hand, he might make it. He's quieter than most. I'm still trying to figure him out. You?"

She cut into another tomato. "I don't know with Shameka. Do you remember when we discussed transferring people to different homes, if they would take them, for situations like this?"

"Yeah."

"I think she'd be better off at a women's shelter."

"Have you talked to her about it?"

"I've hinted but I couldn't read her."

Demetris added the onions to a bowl and placed it alongside the other salad fixings. "How's Noah coming along?"

"I'm not sure. But the things he said during his interview, I doubt he meant to say all that, but it did little to dissuade me from taking him in. It's like the Lord tapped me on the shoulder and nudged me. Before I came in here, I found him on the back porch, rocking."

"What were you doing out there?"

"Making my rounds. I was going to say something, but the hurt expression on his face stopped me. I sat and rocked with him. I think he feels alone."

"And you don't want anyone to feel alone."

There was a ping in her heart. "No. We all want to know we matter. To know someone is there." Even her.

"You know you're not alone too, right, Mercy?"
Demetris tossed the salad and gathered the tomatoes she
cut, placing them on the counter. "You got this. Even
though your family doesn't support you. You know that,
right? You're not alone. God's got your back and so do I."

She gave a small smile and nodded. "Thank you, my
friend. God was telling me the same thing this morning.
I'm not sure what I'm going to do if you ever leave this
place."

"Don't be throwing me to the curb just yet. You're
stuck with me for now."

"I'll take it."

Mercy finished helping Demetris in the kitchen, and
at six o'clock, dinner was served. The buffet line moved at
a quick pace. She made it a point to speak to everyone by
name, and the man of her thoughts was up next. "Hi,
Noah."

Avoiding her gaze, he continued to fill his plate.
"Hey."

"Have a good night, okay?"

With a tilt of his head, he regarded her, then nodded
before moving down the line.

Something she'd felt earlier as she read scripture, and
certainly now, nestled within her mind. She needed to
start praying for this man more while he was here.

Later that night as she finished her security rounds,
Noah was waiting at her door. "Mercy."

She blinked, surprised to find him there. "Did you
need something?"

His mouth grew taut, it opened and closed, then

opened again. "I ... I wanted to thank you for earlier. On the porch."

She smiled inwardly. *He might make it here after all.* "It's a hard world out there. But you're not alone, Noah." She felt for the man and what it took to admit what he had. "You have your job interview tomorrow?"

"I do."

"If you need a ride after breakfast, Tucker, one of our volunteers at the soup kitchen, can drop you off. Please, don't be late."

He nodded before slipping into his room.

"Goodnight," she whispered, locking the bedroom door behind her. "Lord, was that a breakthrough? Please, let it be, and allow me one with Shameka."

CHAPTER 5

𝒩 oah leaned against the counter at the soup kitchen and glanced around the empty facility. He inhaled a deep breath.

In the month since he moved in, he'd become familiar with the routine of the house. Breakfast was served promptly at seven, lunch was served at the soup kitchen from eleven to twelve in the afternoon, and dinner was served back at the house from six to seven in the evening. Everyone was responsible for their personal upkeep, rooms, and laundry. Residents weren't allowed to congregate in the hallways but in the two living room areas. Demetris assisted Mercy with random room checks once a week. And lights-out was promptly at eleven every night.

And Noah knew something else—after that porch encounter with Mercy three weeks ago, he'd decided to make a go of it at the house. So, here he was in the kitchen, waiting to talk with Demetris to follow through on his decision.

Why? Because of Mercy.

He'd seen her every day since, working tirelessly, cooking alongside Demetris, training Tucker to use what he was learning at the university in real-life situations, and she gave constant support to the residents. Especially him.

Mercy reminded him of his late wife. Not physically, but the same compassion, the same love for others that had run through Bella's veins, he found in Mercy. It was bittersweet to long for what he'd lost, to relive the memories and the fact he wasn't home the night the forest fire ripped through the area. Over the past two years, nothing had calmed the turmoil raging within his soul—the anger toward God—or the pain that left his heart broken. Until now. He was like King Saul from the Bible, desperate for David to play the harp to ease the demons within his mind. Mercy was his David. She soothed him, calmed his weary heart. Brought sleep at night.

"You daydreaming?" Demetris shot him a smile as he entered the kitchen. "I heard you wanted to speak to me." He opened a cabinet and withdrew several aluminum pans.

Noah straightened. "I'd like to help out in the kitchen."

Demetris continued to the pantry and withdrew four, ten-pound bags of potatoes. He sauntered to the sink and began opening the bags. "I thought you were hired with Jefferson's Painting." He began washing off the potatoes and glanced at the clock on the wall. "Don't tell me you got fired for not getting a cut and shave. Believe me, Mercy will have something to say about it."

She would. She'd mentioned it in passing a few times

since he'd been hired. Everyone knew Mercy was kind but strictly followed protocol, and being fired was cause for being kicked out of the house. No matter how much he hated being bushwhacked, it left him little choice. "No. I'm still there. I have until the end of the week to get a haircut."

"And you want to work in the kitchen instead of relaxing?"

"I work part-time and clock in at two in the afternoon. There's extra time on my hands that I don't need."

Demetris paused and turned dark eyes toward him. Understanding dawned in his keen gaze. "How long have you been clean?"

"Almost three years."

"Impressive, especially for a man on the streets." Demetris turned back to the job at hand and opened another bag. "Can you cook?"

"It's been a while." Each Wednesday night he'd helped cook for at least a hundred people. The fifty to sixty that showed up here each day for lunch couldn't be that difficult. He hoped.

"It's like ridin' a bike. You like washin' dishes?"

"If it eats up my free time, I'm game. I don't care what it is."

"Then you'll take Mercy's spot. I'll see you tomorrow at eight in the morning."

"Appreciate it," Noah said, giving a nod as he left the kitchen. It was good for him to stay busy, and if it helped Mercy, he was more than glad to do it.

Heading to his room, Noah caught sight of the paramedic who'd assisted him when he first arrived. He was talking with Mercy in the empty living room. Most residents were working or in their rooms, so all he heard as he neared were whispers. When they saw him, he nodded and kept on walking. It was none of his business, but it was obvious the man had a thing for Mercy. Poor guy. If he didn't push too hard, he might have a shot. It was how Noah won Bella over. It was the little things that caught her eye, caring about what she cared about, not the grand gestures or dominating conversations. It was the give and take of their relationship, one he missed with each breath.

Collecting his wallet from the dresser, he closed the door behind him and locked his room. He was running a few minutes behind, so he needed to hurry to make up the time.

Noah strolled past the living room a final time, catching Mercy's pleading eyes. He kept on walking, but as he reached the door, he paused.

Did she need interference? Had he misinterpreted the moment? He was a homeless man. Who cared what he thought?

Noah turned back and strolled up to them, ignoring Brad's strained expression. "Mercy, do you have a few minutes to drive me to work? I was talking with Demetris about helping out in the kitchen, and it took longer than I expected."

She gave a curt nod. "I'll grab my keys. Wait here. I'll meet you in a minute." She walked toward her room without a backward glance.

So he stood there, meeting the frustrated man's gaze. The silence stretched between them.

"Tell Mercy I left. I'll be back." Brad marched his way out just as Mercy rounded the corner.

Without hesitation or a word, she led Noah to her silver sedan. They both slid in, and with the close of the doors, she finally spoke. "Noah, you need a haircut by the end of the week. I can't babysit you like I do the others in this house. You're a capable man, and I'm glad you want to take on more responsibility around here, but if you can't do what I'm asking—"

"I'll have Betty cut it."

The short drive was awkwardly silent until she pulled up to the paint store and parked. She picked up where they left off. "If you need help around the ears, let me know. Betty … sometimes she gets too close or doesn't cut enough, but she's all we have and we're grateful."

He nodded and got out of the car.

"Noah?"

"Yeah." He ducked his head to see her inside the vehicle.

"You could have walked here within minutes, so … thank you."

"Sure." There was nothing like getting reprimanded and thanked in the same breath, but she did need the out, and he was glad to be the one to do it.

Carrying her calendar, Mercy went to the dining room and opened the black spiral notebook to check when the interior designer would arrive. She had to find a bedroom space for herself some place other than in the same hallway as her residents. She should have started this project when she remodeled the first floor. All she could do now was stall her father and give the designer more time to make the attic livable.

A small knock sounded, and Mercy turned to Felicity, who held up the soup kitchen's keys as she approached.

"I appreciate you locking up today," Mercy said.

"No problem." Felicity set the keys on the table. "Hey. Did you see Noah? He still hasn't cut his hair or shaved."

"Yes, I noticed, but it's his choice if he plans to stay on with us or not. He's been working for Jefferson Painting for a little over a month now. He knows the rules. He's no different than Shameka, who constantly breaks curfew."

"Oh, there's a big difference between Shameka and Noah."

"There might be, but neither is abiding by the rules."

"Give them more time."

"How much time? With Shameka, no matter how much I talk with her, my words fall on deaf ears. Even last month, after we had a breakthrough and that tough exterior cracked, I found myself back to square one."

"At least she's still here."

"But for how long?" Mercy closed her calendar and met Felicity's gaze. "Demetris told me there was a man who stopped by looking for her."

"I heard the same. He told the guy not to come back, right?"

"He did, but I'm afraid she won't be able to stay away from her old life much longer. If that's the case, I've done all I can do. I've prayed for her and will continue, but ultimately, it's her choice. I can only give people options to their situation and hope they want a better future. It's the same with Noah."

"I know you're right. I just wish …"

"It's hard pouring your life into people and seeing nothing in return."

"Yeah." Felicity shrugged, eyes downcast. "Real hard. I'll see you tomorrow."

Mercy understood the way Felicity was feeling. But it was Jesus who reminded Mercy that He understood more than anyone during those nights when she poured her heart out to Him over the people staying with her. How she wanted a better life for them, but mostly for them to see Jesus and know of His love.

Time would tell if Shameka and Noah stayed.

She prayed they would.

CHAPTER 6

*N*oah finished scrubbing clean the last of the dishes and wiped his brow with his sleeve. He was exhausted and covered in baked-on food. It felt good. He'd been busy since eight this morning, but it came with a sense of accomplishment that had been lacking in his life for much too long, a feeling that pushed and encouraged him to his next job.

Something else he'd become aware of—if it weren't for Mercy and Demetris running a tight ship, none of this would have been possible. The soup kitchen served a hundred more people than Noah had first thought, and the food they had provided seemed to multiply and went that much further.

Whistling a tune Noah didn't recognize, Tucker walked past. "Has anyone seen Mercy? I can't find her anywhere. My professor sent her an email about a case study she needs to look over."

"No problem," Demetris said, putting away several

pans. "I can relay the message to her. She'll get to what needs to be done."

"Thank you." Tucker lingered a few moments. "Tell her I said hello and missed her today."

Noah turned his face to hide a smile as he washed his hands. The boy was smitten.

"I want in on it." Demetris came to him. "What's with the grin?"

Noah glanced in Tucker's direction as the boy went to Felicity. "Seems our young friend has a crush."

"I'm not sure he's the only one." The man's slightly amused, penetrating look coiled apprehension through Noah's chest.

"No." Noah backed away from the sink. "What you see is admiration and nothing more."

"Are you sure?"

He cared for Mercy. They'd talked a couple of times about her vision for the house. He wanted to see her heart's desire for the community come to fruition. With the right man at her side, she could do so much more. Someone to pray for her, to be an encourager when things looked bleak, or a second hand whenever she needed it, but that man wasn't him. He'd left that profession.

A stilted laugh escaped him as he lifted innocent hands. "Positive."

Eyebrow cocked, Demetris gave him a nod and strolled off to where Felicity and Tucker cleaned tables. A nicely dressed woman in a white pantsuit and heels passed Noah in the kitchen. She glanced around, seemingly lost. Noah was about to ask if he could help her, but when she turned to him and smiled, his breath caught.

"Mercy?"

A puzzled expression furrowed her brows. "Who else?"

Long gone was the daily ponytail and somewhat baggy clothes. Before him stood a completely made-over woman who seemed to have just stepped out of Saks Fifth Avenue.

"You can stop staring. I know I look different. Two hours' worth of different. Do you know where Demetris is? I need to let him know I'm leaving."

Noah cleared his throat and pointed to the dining area. "Over there." He looked away, but only for a second before his gaze returned to her as she hurried off in designer heels.

Demetris gave a wide grin at seeing her, as did Felicity, but Tucker gaped, probably much like Noah had. Mercy was breathtaking. Her hair was like silk, curled down her back and over her shoulders. Her pantsuit accented curves he hadn't known existed. Realizing he was studying her a little too long, he looked away.

It had been years since he'd gawked at a woman who wasn't his wife. He had eyes only for her, but today was different. He wasn't sure how to feel taking an interest in someone else. It was foreign but natural. Day by day, it seemed like everything regarding Mercy, seeing her, being together, was becoming more natural.

Snatching a rag and cleaner from the closet, he finished scrubbing his work area.

Whoever she was having lunch with was a lucky man.

At the thought, a tendon in his neck twitched. He glanced up and caught Demetris eyeing him, his brow cocked. Noah was getting tired of seeing that amused expression on his face.

Mercy parked her sedan and glanced up at The Lighthouse. Her lunch with her father hadn't gone as planned. Dad had reminded her to never put all her eggs in one basket, but that was precisely what she had done. She was all-in financially, mentally, physically, and spiritually. It was all for God. She could not fail. Right?

So why had her father's words made her doubt herself? It was always the same. He'd tempt her with the world she was born in, a world she missed from time to time, but repeatedly, her heart called her elsewhere. Why couldn't he understand her desire to help people, as if it weren't a worthy cause?

She locked the car and quietly entered the house. It was later than she'd planned to return, but her father had planted too many questions and so much doubt about her future that she needed to clear her head before making her way home.

Home.

Her father was right. This wasn't the type of home she had ever imagined, being in her thirties living with destitute men and women. But surely God would see fit to bring someone into her life.

She unlocked her bedroom door and opened it slowly, knowing what was on the other side. What did her father call The Lighthouse? A jail cell? She flicked on the lights, and her stomach soured. The only thing her small room was missing were bars in place of walls.

She set her Gucci bag on the twin bed and slipped off her heels, setting each one back in the box where she stored them.

Lord, I'm feeling overwhelmed. I feel like I'm not enough, and right now, I'm so alone.

A soft knock sounded behind her.

Noah stood in her doorway, dressed in red plaid pajama pants and a white T-shirt that pulled across his chest. She bought every resident five sets of clothing after they arrived, one outfit for work, three for everyday wear, and one for bed. When Noah first came to stay, he was a bit thin, but over the last months, he'd filled out. Thanks to Demetris' cooking and Susan's knowledge for all things medical, Noah looked good.

Healthy, Mercy. He looks healthy.

"Hey, Noah. Everything all right?" She collected her shoe box and slid it back underneath the bed, pushing it farther with her foot.

"I could ask you the same question. I was heading in for the night and went to shut my door and heard you sigh. A few times, as a matter of fact."

She didn't doubt it, the way she was feeling. "I didn't mean to disturb you. I have a lot on my mind. You've met my dad?" *Who hadn't?*

"Briefly."

She withdrew her wallet, hairbrush, and compact from her purse and set them aside on the bed. "We had lunch."

"Lunch? It's almost ten at night. Should I even ask how it went?"

"If I remain silent, does it count as answering?" She slid her purse under the bedframe.

"Do you want to talk about it?"

At the offer, she looked up and met sincerity in his gaze. Why was it when she spoke, it seemed as if he was listening, truly listening, and that her words mattered? But he was the one she wanted to talk about. They rarely had time for the two of them to talk alone, and she wasn't ready for bed with everything on her mind. "How about a compromise? We both share."

His eyes flicked away, then returned to hers. "Okay."

"I'll meet you in the kitchen. Five minutes?"

He nodded and left her doorway.

With a calming breath, she shut the door and changed out of her pantsuit into yoga pants and a large T-shirt. When she entered the kitchen, Noah was waiting at a table, and her heart gave a little flutter. She headed for the fridge. "Hungry?" She took out the ham, cheese, and mayonnaise, and went to the cabinet for bread.

"It's after ten. Isn't it against the rules?" The lift of his mouth was small, hidden behind his beard, but his eyes … they were expressive when he smiled. He was teasing. She liked this side of him.

"I'll let you in on a little secret," she whispered. "I tend to be a rule breaker from time to time."

"You? That can't be possible."

His chuckle warmed her insides, and she found her gaze lingering. "Can I interest you in a sandwich?" Why was there such a pull to him? She'd made the mistake of telling Felicity as much shortly after Noah's brief visits to the soup kitchen last year. Mercy never thought he'd return, but here they were, making sandwiches together.

"So why did you look lost earlier?"

Is that the way I looked? At times she felt lost. Especially after visiting with her dad. "My father doesn't support my lifestyle, and I can't help him understand." Mercy pointed to one of the tables. "Want to sit?"

He followed and sat across from her. "He's not supporting you?"

"This really isn't his thing." She gestured about her. "The home, the homeless."

"Then what you need is a community partner. Several with deep pockets would be better." He took a bite of his sandwich.

It was the reason for her visit with her father today. The lecture about putting all her eggs in one basket, a basket with many holes. She would soon need to be donating her own money to sustain the programs. Grants weren't enough any longer. Needing to change the subject, she took a bite of her sandwich. "Who are you, Noah? Besides the stranger, Noah Peter Allen, within our midst. The man with three first names. You don't fit the model of a homeless man."

"How so?"

"You had showered sometime that day you blacked out. You keep your nails cut and clean. You trim your long beard—which should have been cut off by now. You're a puzzle and too many pieces are missing. I've asked you this before, but why are you here?"

"I didn't realize you were keeping tabs on me. To

answer your questions again, I'm a wanderer. Trying to find my way."

So was every other homeless person she met. *Is he trying to convince me?* "Something you said has been bothering me. You made a comment about my father. How did you know he was wearing Armani?"

His smile stretched a bit too tightly. "I know fashion?"

She fingered the crust of her sandwich. "Somehow, that doesn't ring true."

He turned serious. "I used to own several suits. Armani has the best custom suiting service."

"Now, that rings true. My father mentioned the same." This man had money, or once did. She ate another bite though she was no longer hungry. Her mind began to race. "Are you one of my father's friends playing a part to dissuade me from being here? Like I told him today—"

"No. I don't know your father, and if I did, we might have words. There needs to be more people like you." He looked to his hands, pausing. "My wife, she was like you. Hopeful. Believed in the impossible. She'd always say, 'I'm going to love people the way Jesus loves me,' and she did, no exception. Until the night a forest fire swept through the area where we lived."

Wife ... like you ... fire?

"I wasn't home when it happened." His voice cracked.

Mercy couldn't believe what she was hearing. Instinctively, she reached over and covered his hand. "Where were you?"

He swallowed. "Getting help."

"Did you find someone?"

"Not the way you're thinking." His jaw clenched, a range of emotions flickered through his features. "I had a car accident a while back, and the hospital prescribed pain meds. I never thought … I'd become addicted. I had an appointment the day of the fire with my therapist. Bella and I knew there was a chance the fire would spread with the winds, but we never thought—" He clenched his hand and swallowed. "Bella insisted I go and not miss my appointment. I hadn't had a pill in three months, but I'd been struggling. She knew it. She always knew. Bella said they'd be fine." The muscle in his jaw tightened, and his throat bobbed.

They? Her chest burned with the truth. *Please, Lord …*

"My wife and son, they died in the fire. They were trying to escape but didn't make it out."

There were no words. Not enough sorrys in this world to bring his family back or heal his heart, so she gripped his hand tighter, hoping to bring some comfort for all he'd been through. It was nothing in comparison, but it was all she could offer with this maddening pull to comfort him. This pull, it was uncalled for, unwanted, but nevertheless it was there, and it was time to distance herself.

She removed her hand and took their plates to the kitchen and dumped their half-eaten sandwiches in the trash. Noah came up to her, his gray eyes watery.

"I'll wash." He brushed her hand as he took the plates and set them in the sink. "I'm a master washer now. Let me show you my skills." He collected a rag from the drawer and turned the water on.

"How long has it been?" she whispered, feeling as if she was intruding.

"They've been gone for over two years." His voice was low, tired sounding all of a sudden. "Some days are easier. Others, I can't wait until the Lord takes me."

Mercy stared at his back in disbelief. His words. She didn't know how it happened, but she felt something for this man. She blinked back her own tears and turned away. "I can't imagine. I'm so sorry." She had to get out of there before she made a complete mess of things. Sometimes she was so easy to read, and now wasn't the time for Noah to learn this about her. "I think I'll head to bed. Good night."

"Mercy, wait." His hand caught hers. "There's more you should know ..." He anchored his gaze to her watery eyes. "Are those tears?"

She couldn't deny them. She said nothing.

He studied her face for a long moment, then his gaze sank to her mouth.

Another second ticked by before she forced a step away from his touch. "Can you make sure the dishes get put away? We don't want Demetris to know we were in the kitchen after hours."

"I'd hate for that to happen. Sometimes rule makers need a break from their own policies, even if it's only for a short time."

A dim smile faded on her lips as she left him.

If she wasn't careful, she'd break the biggest rule of all.

CHAPTER 7

*M*ercy turned off the last of the soup kitchen's lights and headed to her office to collect her things.

Demetris appeared at her door. "Are you ready?"

"Hey, you." She flicked off the office light, then shouldered her bag. "You don't always have to wait on me."

He crossed his muscular arms and lifted a dark brow, leveling her with one of his stares that made people shudder. "What kinda friend would I be if I didn't? This is no place for you to be alone."

"All right." She smiled. "Come on."

"So when is the woman coming to look at the attic?" Demetris locked the front door behind them.

"In about an hour. It will give me enough time to wash up. I can't imagine having my own place again, especially a bathroom. I hope she can manage it."

"If she can't, I told you I don't mind trading spaces. It never felt right taking your place."

"You needed quiet at nights since you were taking

online classes, and I had the perfect spot. Besides, I'm a heavy sleeper. Once my head hits the pillow, I'm out before I know it."

"That's not good."

The strain in his voice brought her attention to him. "What? Falling asleep so quickly?"

"Shameka."

Mercy's gaze found what Demetris had seen— Shameka carrying a suitcase to a dark vehicle parked at the side of the house. The trunk popped open, and she threw her suitcase inside and slammed the trunk.

"Shameka!" Mercy called, hurrying toward her.

Shameka opened the passenger side door and looked in her direction. The woman paused, and Mercy thought for a moment she might change her mind, but in the next breath, she slid into the car and shut the door. By the time Mercy and Demetris made it to The Lighthouse, Shameka was gone.

Mercy stood in the yard, hurt and angry, staring in the direction they had driven off. She wanted to call Shameka back, tell her not to go, plead her case, but like she told Felicity not long ago, everyone had a choice. Shameka had made hers. Mercy's heart moaned.

Demetris touched her elbow. "Come on," he murmured. "There's nothing more you can do."

He was right, of course, but a part of her rebelled against the idea. She should have done more. Somehow. Someway. But what? With a heavy breath, she followed Demetris inside.

～

Noah heard a commotion in the hallway. He tried not to get involved, but he was growing fond of those in the house. By the time he decided to look, Shameka was walking out the front door with a suitcase.

A few women stood in the hallway chattering, but Marylou, one of the younger women nearest to him, tsked and rolled her eyes. "I can't believe she's goin' back to him. What a loser." She pushed her way through the other ladies and headed to her room.

Noah felt sorry for Marylou. By the way she and Shameka had talked and shared smiles, it was obvious they'd built a friendship. In a place like this, it was important to connect with someone. Now, that person was gone for Marylou.

His heart panged for Mercy too. How would she handle the news?

She and Demetris entered the house a second later. Their long faces said they knew about Shameka. Mercy was the first to speak to the group in the hallway. "Ladies, everyone here has a choice, and sometimes, people choose to move on."

"Or go back to their pimp," voiced Val, one of the reformed street women.

Sadness flittered across Mercy's features. "Whatever the reason Shameka left, I hope you know my door is always open."

Aiyden, the man who roomed across the hall from Noah, came out looking a little bleary-eyed. Since moving in, Noah had rarely seen him. "Y'all know I work the night shift. Can you go back to where you came from? I need my beauty sleep."

"Aiyden," Demetris piped up, "if that's what you call beauty, you need a year's worth of sleep." He and Val laughed and spun to go in the opposite direction.

"Sorry they woke you," Mercy said, face unreadable as she unlocked her room. "Maybe you can get back to sleep."

"I'm sure I can." Aiyden looked to Noah. "How's it going, neighbor? Getting used to the house?"

Mercy disappeared into her room, and the door closed behind her. How Noah wished he could follow her there to be a sounding board. It was the least he could do. "Getting there. Where do you work?"

"Hospital maintenance. At first it was hard adjusting to working the night shift. I asked Mercy to find me another job. She said no. I'm glad she did. I wouldn't trade it now for anything. Well, I should get back to bed. Later."

Noah stepped into his room, but as he was closing the door, there was a gentle knock. He found the woman who'd captured his thoughts over the last two days standing there. "Mercy."

"I hope I'm not bothering you, but didn't you say you worked in construction?"

Was she looking for him to start a job on a construction site instead of the paint store? Because if that was the case, he'd have to come clean about which job had actually qualified him to list "construction" on his application. The only requirement needed for him to get the job was being able-bodied. He'd always qualified for that, helping to set drywall, sledgehammer through walls, use a paint brush, fix a leaking toilet ... on-the-job training came in handy.

"I can see your hesitation," she rushed on, "and I understand after picking up more hours in the kitchen, but I need an extra set of eyes on a project. I was hoping you might be able to help in your free time."

"You're asking me to oversee a project?"

"Like a foreman, but you wouldn't have to lift a finger."

Demetris stuck his head around the corner. "Mercy, they're here."

"Tell them I'm coming." She looked back to Noah. "What do you say?"

Knowing how important this project was to her, he could watch it unfold. He had enough experience. "Sure. Why not?"

"Great. Let's go."

"Where to?" He stood there gaping as she smiled at him.

"With me. We have a meeting to go to."

He followed but couldn't keep his thoughts from bouncing from Mercy's beautiful smile to how much he missed his wife. How much he needed her. The Lord knew he'd give up his life in the blink of an eye for his family to still be alive. Yet, the other night, at seeing the tears in Mercy's eyes, his heart tugged in a different direction. His steps faltered. An emotion he was afraid to name strangled his throat.

He hurried to follow Mercy, and when she introduced him to a man and woman sitting at one of the kitchen tables, all he could do was nod.

"Thank you for coming," Mercy said, pulling out her chair. "What do you think? Is it feasible?"

Noah sat alongside her, fighting to keep his focus on the here and now, but his mind found its way back to Bella. He missed her something fierce in the quiet of the nights, the feel of her next to him, especially now that he was sleeping in a bed again. It was the reason he preferred the streets. Asphalt and concrete against his flesh was uncomfortable, and having nowhere to go, he could walk until his eyes grew heavy, keeping his thoughts of Bella from reaching his dreams.

"Noah." Mercy nudged his leg under the table. "Isn't that right?"

"Yes," he said mechanically.

"Good," the man agreed. "Let's take a final look at the attic, and I'll walk you through what we plan to do."

Everyone stood.

Noah glanced toward the door. He bit back the bitter taste in his mouth and lagged behind them as his body went into cruise control up to the attic. As a foreman, he should be focusing on what was being said, but all he wanted to do was grab his things and walk back to Tennessee. To lie on the property that once was his home. Bella was slipping further away from him with Mercy around, and he couldn't let that happen.

A gentle pressure touched his hand, and he jerked. Remembering where he was, he blinked his vision clear to find Mercy's sorrowful gaze on him.

"It's okay," she whispered.

But it wasn't. The way she gazed into his eyes, searching. The way he wanted to move that rebel hair from her face and …

She wasn't Bella.

He left her with them and climbed down out of the attic. Once in his room, he withdrew his backpack from under the twin bed and stuffed his things inside. Within minutes he walked out the door much like Shameka had. Maybe for people like them, a second chance, a new life, was more frightening than breaking free from the sins of the past.

"Noah, where are you going?"

He slowed his steps to a stop but couldn't bear the idea of looking at her, seeing the questions in Mercy's eyes. She'd done so much for him, more than he'd ever admit.

"Noah." She was right behind him now.

He turned toward Mercy's gentle voice, fighting to go. Fighting to stay. "It's time."

She stood so close, and those beautiful brown eyes sought his for answers. "Why?" she finally voiced in a low murmur. "I don't understand. Did I do something? Say something?"

"It's just time for me to go home."

She frowned slightly. Her expression said she knew the answer. "Tennessee?"

He dipped his head in acknowledgement.

"I guess I've always known you'd be leaving."

"How?"

"You never wanted to shave. Those who don't normally leave before their time is up. It's why I pushed you so hard."

Mercy wanted him to stay? She had no clue what she did to him. How alive she made him feel. How at peace he was in her presence. He didn't deserve it. "You were right." His shoulders fell. "Bye, Mercy."

As he was nearing the final block, he glanced back and found Mercy still standing there, watching him. She was a lovely sight even from where he stood. One he'd sorely miss.

She started walking toward him.

What was the stubborn woman doing? Unable to resist, he met her halfway. "Mercy."

"Don't go."

"I'm restless. Confused."

"You mean wrestling with the past?"

"With what I've lost …" He looked to his feet. "I need to go home. If only to mourn again. It's hard to be away."

"Your family?"

"Yes." The strength it took to admit his need, to look back into her gaze, zapped the meager energy he carried. He shifted his backpack.

"Will you be back?"

He felt it then, the weight of her question, the time he'd spent here—with her. A question he couldn't answer.

"I'll be praying for you, Noah. And for safe travels."

"Thank you, Mercy. And in case our paths don't cross again, your name … it suits you."

CHAPTER 8

*A*s Noah took those final steps up the incline of his road, he saw an area being restored to its previous glory with new family homes and rentals. The marks of a fire were almost invisible, but the burns to his soul hadn't faded so quickly. The memories of Bella and their son continued to draw him home no matter where he roamed. But with each step he took away from Mercy, an entirely new battle waged. He hadn't wanted to leave her.

Mercy was a surprise. Her gentle spirit and determined care for others made him miss his old life as a pastor. A life and ministry he could never resurrect because of his past sins, the reason he drove away the day of the fire to deal with his addiction. The reason his wife and son died.

He entered the gated yard where he once lived and pushed his way up the long drive. How many times had he walked this concrete to carry the trash to the curb and roll it up the next day? Hundreds. It wasn't enough.

Noah looked over their charred yard and fixed his eyes on their home, where only the slab remained. Moisture filled his gaze as he walked through where the door had once been.

"Bella ... *I'm home.*" He closed his eyes, imagining her smile, her kiss. Though the taste of her had faded as had the smell of her perfume, that smile was forever engraved in his mind and heart.

Noah trudged his way down to a few trees the fire hadn't licked and dropped his backpack to the ground. He withdrew a blanket and their old hammock and tied it up. He climbed in and closed his eyes, then listened to the birds as dusk began to fall.

He was home.

Mercy had signed the contracts for the attic remodeling. Although construction wouldn't begin for another week, she was getting a jumpstart on removing her things from the attic in hopes it would keep her mind off Noah. The problem was, Demetris insisted on helping her move. They were getting things done more quickly than anticipated. When he suggested putting her things in Noah's old room, what else could she do but agree?

In the weeks since Noah left, Mercy had found herself waking up at odd hours of the night, praying for him, sometimes even in the middle of the day. Her mind would start to race, and worry would snatch her breath. It had never been like this before with one of her residents, and it scared her, but Noah was different. She should have spoken to Demetris about it long ago, to help her pray. But every time she thought of what to say, it sounded crazy to tell him of her feelings for a homeless man who'd left her.

Even now, as she sorted attic clutter, she struggled to concentrate.

"How old is this?" Demetris held up a ceramic figurine of a girl with brown hair in a pink dress with a puffy hat.

Mercy smiled, remembering holding her mother's hand as they'd entered the pottery shop for their weekly trips. "Mom used to love making ceramics. She helped me make this one and pick the colors. As you can tell, pink was my favorite."

"I'm glad your color choices have changed." He gave her a sideways smile, holding the ceramic against his wide chest, as if it were a child. One day he'd be a wonderful, loving husband and father. Her heart leaped to Noah.

"Where do you want her?" Demetris asked.

She glanced around, hiding the emotion he'd easily spot on her face. If there was anyone who knew her well, it was him. "On top of the dresser is fine." As her gaze roamed the back of the attic, she spotted a set of lamps she'd been hunting, but there were no shades.

Demetris cleared his throat as he rummaged through a torn box. "Mercy?"

"Yeah. Did you find another hidden treasure?" She went to where she saw the lamps, and on the way, fingered a clear bin that held her mother's china.

"Do you have feelin's for Noah?"

Mercy paused, her throat constricting at the sound of

his name. She should have known Demetris had witnessed her feelings, no matter how hard she tried to hide them. She spent more time with him than anyone, and their friendship rivaled that of her own family's. More so because of his sacrifice to help her shoulder the responsibility of the house.

A minute ticked by, and she'd yet to respond. How could she when her heart and mind battled these feelings knowing she might never see Noah again? Thankful she was hidden from view by the boxes, she hoped her voice didn't give anything away. "What do you mean?"

"You haven't been the same since he left."

She retrieved the set of lamps and came from behind the boxes. "It's not only him, but Shameka. I lost two people in the same day. You know how much time I invest in the lives of those who are here, and they both just walked out and left. I admit, it hurt. Still hurts."

"And Noah?"

She set the lamps down and looked to the ceramic child in his arms. "What about him?"

"Girl, come on. You won't even look at me because you know it's true." He switched the child to the other arm. "Who do you think you're talkin' to here? I knew you had a thing for him. I thought with time you'd open up, but you've been so close-lipped. I need to make sure you're all right. You finally let someone in, and he leaves."

She looked to the ground. It was true. All of it. Demetris knew her. She could trust him, be herself without judgment of how truly foolish her heart was. "I can't tell you how it happened. I wish I could explain it away, but yes, there were feelings. I'm afraid there still are."

Demetris nodded numerous times as if absorbing her admission. "Have you heard from him?"

"No. I don't think I will." She swallowed around the throbbing of her heart, the yearning to see him again. "The last we spoke he was set on going home. I got the impression he planned to stay." She tried not to dwell on their last moments and the reason she needed to keep busy. She looked around for the lamp shades.

"Maybe this isn't a good time to tell you, but Brad stopped by yesterday."

"I know." She gave him a sheepish grin. "I hid in the bathroom while you spoke." Finding the shades, she told Demetris where they were.

"Mercy." He nibbled on the corner of his lip and flashed her an irritated look.

They traded glances. "I told you before that ship not only sailed but sank."

"Then think about accepting your father's invite to his annual party. It's still two months away."

"You know he's only trying to set me up with someone in hopes I'll fall in love and leave this place."

His voice softened. "Would it be so bad to meet someone? Who knows, you might find Mr. Right under all that money. Someone who likes to get his hands dirty."

She looked to the ceramic child in his arms, the endearing image it made. "I want to believe there's a man out there for me—one who wants to make a difference in the world." *One who will love me and stay.*

"They'd be lucky to find you, Mercy Grace Cunningham. Think about it." Demetris climbed down the stairs.

She followed him carefully, carrying both lamps. At the second to last step from the floor, one was taken from her. She turned to find Brad holding the lamp.

"Let me help." He extended his other hand for the second one.

She gave it to him. "I wasn't expecting you."

Brad set the lamps on the floor by the room. "No, you wouldn't when you're a hard woman to find. Any other man would think you were ignoring him." Disappointment shrouded his face as they stood in the hallway.

Demetris walked by and clapped him on the shoulder. "Maybe that's because you don't take hints very well." He took to the stairs behind them.

Mercy pinched her lips together to keep from smiling. "What can I do for you?"

"We never finished our conversation."

And she thought she'd made herself more than clear. Demetris came down with the lamp shades. "Brad and I will be outside," she told him. "Take a break. We can work on it more when I get back."

Marylou walked by the room, then backpedaled, eyeing what was inside. "You's got a lot of stuff. You havin' a yard sale or somethin'?"

"Moving my things. They'll be working on the attic soon."

"If you ever want to unload this stuff, I can do it for ya."

Marylou was known as Ms. Pawn in the neighborhood. She used to pawn everything she stole. It was how she got caught and landed here two years ago. But she was a loyal bear when it came to protecting and caring for those in the house.

"Thank you, Marylou, but I'm good."

The woman gave her a nod before turning her attention to Brad. "Don't be comin' in here givin' Miss Mercy any trouble." She pointed a long fingernail in his direction. "We're family here and—"

"Marylou," Demetris' strong voice interrupted. "Let's go. You can help me prep for dinner."

The woman pointed to her eyes and then back to Brad to indicate she was watching him. When they walked outside, Mercy saw movement at the curtains. It seemed the entire house was on high alert with Brad in the area.

"So what did you want to talk about?" she asked politely, as if she didn't know exactly why he'd come.

He drilled his gaze into hers. "Us. It's always about us. And before we get interrupted, let me say I want another chance."

"We've already been through this. It's not going to happen."

"Because you won't let it. How about dinner?"

"Brad, I'm sorry, but it's over and has been for a while now. And if you must know, there's someone else."

That quieted him down. She could see the wheels turning.

"You and I are friends now, and that's all we'll ever be."

Mercy waited for him to say something, anything, but

he just glanced toward his truck. Perhaps this was the goodbye he needed. "I wish you well, Brad."

"Who is it?" He turned back to her.

With a saddened heart she said, "He left. It's the way life is, Brad. People come and go. If anyone is fully aware of that fact, it's me," she murmured, turning inward, a truth settling in her bones. "But God has never left. In everything, He sustains and brings me hope. I'll see you around, Brad." She pushed open the door and headed for the attic.

Her life might fit into boxes with not much to show, but she prayed she was leaving a legacy in the lives she touched. That one day, this family as Marylou claimed they were, would be together again—Noah included—if not on this earth, then in Heaven.

CHAPTER 9

*N*oah rose from the hard plywood he used as a mattress and glanced around the half-burned camper at the back of the property. The stench still covered everything and hadn't lightened in the few weeks since he'd returned home. What had changed was him.

At first, he'd attributed the change in mood to the wind that blew in from the south or to his once-loved hammock becoming uncomfortable, but he'd eventually owned up to the truth. His heart was changing no matter how much he tried to hold on to his family and bury the pain. For so long there had been no future, nothing to live for, but at some point, a glimmer of hope had found him. It had taken root under Mercy's care, and no matter how far he traveled, it was growing. And in turn, he wanted more than the life he had now.

The months of watching Mercy work at the house and soup kitchen had brought on a need to help others that he'd not felt since his addiction. But why? He was a tarnished man. The Lord couldn't use him. The church had made that clear when he'd found the courage to speak to the deacons about his drug abuse. They'd immediately released him as pastor and sent him and his family on their way. The fifteen years they'd spent in that church seemed to have meant nothing. It was just another way he'd hurt his wife, a wife who had stood by his side through anything, after everything.

Anger once again caught in his throat. "Lord, I don't understand why you didn't take me." Of the three of them, he was the weakest, the broken one.

Noah got out of bed and headed down to his favorite spot. He hung the hammock, then climbed in.

"Excuse me, sir," came a voice from behind him. "I'm going to have to ask you to leave."

Noah turned to his neighbor, who stood several feet away. "Mark, it's Noah."

"Noah?" he asked, coming toward him. "I thought you were a ... "

Vagrant.

"It's me."

"I didn't recognize you. You look rough."

"Thanks, man."

"I didn't mean ..."

"No worries. I know I do. I'd offer you a seat on the hammock, but it's been a while since I've had a shower."

"Then come to the house. Get washed up. There's something I've been wanting to ask you."

"If it's about the property, I'm still not interested in selling."

"Will you at least hear me out?"

It was the least Noah could do. Mark had taken care

of the seven-acre lot since the day Noah walked away. "You don't think Camille will mind?"

"She'd love to have you."

Noah stood and began unhooking one side of the hammock from the tree while Mark untied the other.

"Oh, and so you know, we've adopted a baby girl. Well, she's not so much a baby anymore."

Noah absorbed the news. They had been on a long journey for this child, and she was finally here. He smiled warmly. "Congratulations. I'm so happy for you. How old is she?" Noah folded the hammock and stuffed it in his backpack. They started for the driveway.

"Almost two. Our pride and joy."

"You both deserve this happiness. After everything."

"And Camille and I have you to thank. When you counseled us, it was during the toughest time in our marriage. After losing our firstborn and being unable to get pregnant again, we were barely hanging on."

"But you made it. God is …" Noah couldn't finish the sentence.

Mark slowed to a stop. "He is good, Noah. When we were thrown into the fire of this life, it killed us. We allowed it to destroy our marriage, but God was there. You showed us He was our Hope, our Comforter, in the worst times of our lives. The way you and Bella were there for us. The Lord used you both. He is good. The Lord is good."

Noah continued toward Mark's black truck over rough gravel and charred limbs, but it was his friend's words that almost made him stumble. The loss of Noah's family had almost buried him alive, just as the death of

Mark and Camille's child nearly destroyed them. His heart wrestled with the pain, the longing for his family, the hope he felt with Mercy, and the truth—that the Lord was indeed good.

Once they reached the vehicle, Mark unlocked the doors, and Noah slid into the passenger seat. "Thank you for inviting me."

"You would have done the same. But there is one condition."

"That is?"

"Maybe two. You've got to shower when we get to the house. But first, roll down your window."

Noah chuckled, pressing the button. The wind whipped through his beard and hair, blowing his stench up his nose. Maybe it was time to cut his hair and shave as Mercy had wanted. Though she'd never see it, he'd give her the one thing he couldn't give until now. "Do you have an extra razor?"

"More than one, and with that beard, you're going to need scissors."

As they continued to drive, Mark spoke about Camille and the expansion of her hair salon and about his own accounting business and this year's completed tax season. He also asked where Noah had traveled since they'd seen each other last. Noah told about his wanderings, but he shared nothing about Mercy. He wasn't ready to speak of her because when he did, or if he did, there was no turning back, and his Bella would slip further away.

~

After bathing and changing, Noah sat on a kitchen barstool and stared at his reflection in the handheld mirror Camille had given him.

"What do you think?" she asked with a broad smile.

He wasn't sure what to say. "I think I'd forgotten what I look like. I'm older than I remembered." He ran a hand down his smooth jaw.

"Just the opposite. You look forty years younger." She went to the closet and came back with a broom. "You hold on to that mirror while I sweep up." She busied herself while Noah took a few more minutes to study his face. He looked so different. He wondered what Mercy would say if she saw him now.

He smiled at the thought, but it faded when he realized how much he wanted to please her.

"Thank you, Camille. It looks great." He stood from the barstool and set the mirror on the table. "I think I'll find Mark."

"Sure thing. He's out back."

Noah found Mark on the deck, looking over the Tennessee mountains. The fire's track was still visible from where they stood. How everything had changed.

"Life slipped through my fingers that day," Noah said.

"I've been praying that with time … maybe the pain would lessen and you'd come home to stay. Rebuild."

"Home is here. This is where my family lies. But lately, I've felt a change."

"Change is good."

Noah looked away and leaned against the deck railing. "I'm not sure how I feel about it."

"How do you mean?"

"I've been in Atlanta at a homeless shelter for several months, and there's a pull to go back there." Noah's thoughts drifted to the first time he saw Mercy. How her brown hair had poked out in different directions from her ponytail. She'd been a mess, but when she'd noticed a man weathered from time and sun, she'd sat next to him and smiled. It was as if the heavens had opened and shone down all around her. He hadn't been able to pull his gaze away.

"Noah?"

"There's a pull, like I need to stay in Atlanta. There, at The Lighthouse."

"Living homeless?"

"No. I don't know."

There was a long silence before Mark shuffled his feet and pointed to the patio furniture. "Let's sit."

Noah rubbed the back of his neck and joined his friend, sitting across from him. "I'm afraid of losing Bella, more than I already have. The idea of living on without her, it feels wrong."

"Noah, Bella and Peter will always be with you. They are a part of you. No matter what the future holds."

"I want to cling to them, to every memory."

"I'm sure Job felt the same."

"The Bible's Job?"

Mark shifted in his seat. "It feels odd talking to you about this. But, yes. I'm sure he was thankful for the time he was given with his children. The Lord restored Job and gave him twice as much as he lost. Maybe the Lord is leading you to a place in your life where He can restore you."

"Job wasn't a drug addict."

"No, but Job wasn't there for his family either at their passing. Sometimes things happen that are out of our control. Have you ever thought maybe God saved you for a purpose?"

"You and I both know that's not true. The church made that perfectly clear."

"So they handled things wrong. They made a mistake, but a church, a group of people, cannot take away the call the Lord has on your life. Only you can."

Noah shook his head. "It wasn't right what they did. Maybe it was, but not the way they did it. I don't know anymore, but I was so hurt. After Bella and Peter died, I became bitter. The pain. The grief. I couldn't endure the fire I was walking through. God took the brunt of my words."

"God can handle it. Nothing you could have said or felt was a surprise. But listen, you did endure, and though you might not have felt Him then, He didn't leave. He walked through that fire right alongside you. Every tear you cried, He saw, and he counted each one. He did the same for Camille and me after our loss."

They sat in silence for some time, and the quietness pushed Noah to look to the future, to a place that hadn't existed a year ago. A hope he hadn't wanted until now. Noah stood. "I think I'm heading up. I appreciate you inviting me to stay the night."

"Noah, you're welcome here as long as you like. I think the Lord is trying to speak to you, and you're wrestling."

"Like Jacob." Noah grinned.

"Yes, my friend. Like Jacob."

Before he turned to leave, Noah asked, "Do you think God can still use a man like me?"

"More than ever. If only you allow Him."

Later that night as Noah lay in bed, he meditated on his friend's words, and tears pricked his eyes. "I don't know who I am anymore. I want to live again. Show me how."

CHAPTER 10

*N*oah couldn't sleep. After watching the alarm clock tick away the hours, he left the guest room and went out onto the deck. The half-moon gave enough light for him to find his way, and he settled into a patio chair.

He missed the quiet of the country and the clean air, the feeling of home, but since his talk with Mark, the cord to Atlanta had become shorter. It was time for him to get back. Not as a homeless man, but as Noah Peter Allen, an ex-addict, ex-pastor, a man who wanted a fresh start and who wanted to help people much like himself.

During the night hours, the Lord brought to his mind the lost people Jesus had helped, the low of the low, the outcasts. Jesus had loved them, fed them, and brought physical and emotional comfort to them. Noah wasn't Jesus, but he could certainly be His hands and feet again. He knew what it was like to be both a mega-church pastor and a homeless man who'd lost everything that mattered. God, by His grace, wasn't finished with him.

Noah now had a purpose, but would Mercy allow him in her life, her heart, and in her ministry?

A creak sounded to his left. Mark came out onto the deck and sank into a chair. "How long have you been up?" He yawned and rubbed his forehead.

Noah noticed for the first time it had gotten lighter around him. "What time is it?"

"Seven."

"I'm not sure if I even went to sleep." He smiled and inhaled a calming breath, enjoying the Lord's blanketing peace and comfort. "I need to leave today."

"For Atlanta?"

"It's time to go. I think you were right. The Lord isn't done using me yet, and not as a homeless man—I'm not destitute—but as a fallen man saved by grace."

"Aren't we all?"

"Amen." Noah leaned back in his chair. "Now, what were you going to ask me? Something about the property?"

"Camille and I would like to know if you plan to rebuild. If not, we'd like to buy two of your acres."

"Which two?"

"The two closest to our house. I know what that would mean for you, so if you say no, I understand. Camille's mom is getting up in years, and we'd like to build on, add a mother-in-law suite."

Noah didn't have to think much on the decision with God's leading so clear in his mind. He smiled. "Of course, you can. After everything, I couldn't have made it through the years without your and Camille's love and support. But I do need someone to drive me around today. Are you up for it? The first stop is the bank."

"Car shopping included?"

He nodded. "And a driver's license. It's been a while since I've driven."

Mark pointed to the house. "Then let's eat. We have a full day ahead of us."

Noah had been on the road for an hour, reminiscing about the love of his life and his precious son. The day he found out Bella was pregnant, she had surprised him by cooking a fancy dinner and placing a wrapped present for him at the table. To his amazement, it was a onesie. She named their son Peter after him because she said he was the cornerstone of their family and pointed them toward Jesus.

Although Noah had struggles, he took his responsibility as husband and father to heart. He would have done anything for them even now, but it seemed the Lord had other plans. He still didn't understand why his loved ones were taken away so early, but God was moving him, pointing him toward a new future.

As he drove and darkness settled around him, his thoughts turned to Mercy. He wanted to be a part of her ministry. Not only her ministry, but her life. How she'd entered his heart was still a mystery, but even across the miles, she was there at every turn—his thoughts of her, that smile of hers, eyes that seemed to search his soul.

Nearing Atlanta, anxiety found him. Or was that

excitement? He wasn't sure what the foreign feeling was, but it certainly seemed like happiness. What would Mercy say when he returned? Would she be happy to see him? Want him there, not as a lost man, but as a man who'd found himself and who wanted a future with her?

Happiness. Noah smiled. The Lord was indeed restoring him.

Noah wasn't sure where to park at the house, so when he arrived, he drove around the block, then parked at the corner of the building near the back entrance.

How should he let her know he was here? He didn't think knocking on the door would work since it was after hours and he looked nothing like the Noah they knew. Previously, he didn't have a cell phone, so he left without her number.

He took a heavy breath and closed his eyes. "Lord, I could sleep in my car."

A door shut in the distance, and Noah opened his eyes. Mercy was leaving? He looked at the time on the car's dashboard. Almost nine at night. Where was she going?

He grabbed his new backpack from the passenger seat, got out of the car, and locked the door. "Mercy?"

When she didn't seem to hear, he dumped his bag on the doorstep and hurried after her.

CHAPTER 11

$\mathcal{T}$he last month since Noah left had been different, and yet, each passing day, her heart grew more toward him. *Where is he, Lord? Why do I have the distinct feeling he needs this place?*

At her desk, Mercy bowed her head, not for Noah this time, but for herself. "I can't do this, Lord, think of him like I am. It's affecting more than my mind."

She opened her eyes and looked at the time on her computer screen. Her father would be calling soon, and the way her mind was flitting elsewhere, it was useless to work on financials tonight.

Mercy glanced around for her phone and noticed it wasn't where she'd left it. Or had she even brought it from her room? She couldn't remember using it since ... yesterday? Impossible.

She headed for the old attic, climbed her new staircase, and unlocked the door to her apartment. She stood in the doorway, and thankfulness filled her heart yet again. Since the contractors had been able to raise the roof, her large floor plan included a living space that led to two bedrooms and a bathroom. Her bedroom, the larger of the two, held a dresser, nightstands, and a queen bed, but it was the spacious full-size bathroom where she spent more of her time, enjoying her freestanding soaker tub. But since the day everything was completed, the only person she wanted to share it with was Noah. She could no longer deny her growing feelings. She dreamt of a future of them in this place as husband and wife.

Mercy pushed her thoughts aside and began searching for her phone. After ten minutes and no cell, she realized there was one place she hadn't checked. The soup kitchen. It was too late for Mercy to head over, but she had to look.

She went downstairs and checked the clock in one of the living rooms. Her father would be calling in twenty-five minutes. She was afraid of what he might do if she didn't answer, and tonight was not the time for a visit.

With her key chain in hand and pepper spray dangling from her wrist, she snuck out of the house. She should have made Demetris aware she was stepping out for a few minutes, but she'd be back before anyone would notice.

Except for the people on the streets.

Day in and day out, she'd forced herself not to dwell on the activity happening at night in this area, but as she walked, darkness seemed to devour her whole.

"Well lookee here. It's Miz Mercy come to grace us with her presence." The voice of a woman she knew called from the alley shadows. A man was wrapped around her thin body.

Oh, Shameka.

"Isn't it past your bedtime, Mercy?" the older man taunted her. "Us grown-ups are about to have some fun." He laughed and turned to Shameka, who hung on his arm. "Isn't that right?"

"You gots it, baby." She chuckled as they made their way to the man's dark sports car.

Mercy couldn't let this opportunity go. It had been weeks since she'd seen her. There'd been talk she'd disappeared, but here she was. "And when you're tired of being used, Shameka, you know where you can find me."

Shameka didn't respond, but Mercy knew she heard her.

The man paused to glare at Mercy as he got in the car. A moment later the car slowly drove off in the opposite direction.

One more block to go. Can you keep your mouth shut long enough to make it? She glanced ahead and noticed for the first time a group of men watching her walk toward them.

One of the men called out to her with a gesture, and her body tightened. This was a mistake, but it was too late to turn around. Picking up her pace, she sensed someone behind her. With each step, she prayed for protection and vowed to never make a fool-hearted decision again, regardless of the consequences with her father.

She reached the door and opened it quickly, but someone pushed her from behind into the building. She grabbed her pepper spray and spun, shooting it directly into a man's face.

He cried out, hunching. "Mercy! It's me, Noah!" He was panting now.

"Noah?" She flipped on the lights by the door. It took a moment for the confusion to clear before she led him to the sink. "Oh, my goodness, Noah! I'm so sorry! Why … how are you—? Stop, don't open your eyes. A few more steps." Once they reached the sink, she turned on the cold water. "Here."

He began splashing his eyes and his—he'd shaved!

She couldn't help but watch him in complete embarrassment and shock. But then, from what she could see, he didn't resemble the Noah she knew. "Are you all right? I'm so sorry. You scared me." She grabbed kitchen towels from the drawer and rushed back to his side. She pushed one into his hand. "Here's a towel."

He rose and moaned as he pressed the towel to one side of his face. The eye she could see was still closed. "I think you missed the left side of my face." The eye opened and met hers.

She tried not to stare, but he looked like a different man. "Let me see." She palmed his hand and moved the towel away from his face. Even with his right eye swelling and redness taking hold, he had to be one of the handsomest men to cross her path. "It doesn't look good."

He gave her a slight smile, the first she'd ever seen without his beard, and her heart fluttered. "Are you talking about the haircut or the eye?" he said.

"The eye, of course." On a nervous chuckle, she released his hand, trying not to stare. "It seems you got a haircut and a shave after all."

"It'll take some getting used to, but if I had waited, maybe the spray wouldn't have been so effective. Glad to know you can wield a can of pepper spray."

"Not good enough. I only got half your face."

"Good thing." His smile lingered, as did her perusal of his strong beardless jawline and the perfect set of his mouth.

She forced herself to look away, mortified at her gawking. "What are you doing here?" Her voice cracked, and she cleared her throat. "Were you following me?"

"I was coming to The Lighthouse and saw you leave. To make sure you were all right, I followed you. When I heard what the men were saying, I needed them to know you weren't alone."

"Noah, that was—" *Her phone?* She hurried to the sound and grabbed her cell from one of the serving stations and answered. "Father."

"Mercy. How are you this evening?"

"I'm doing well." She glanced at Noah, who was now sitting at one of the farthest tables, perhaps to give her some privacy. "Thinking about you."

"I noticed you rescheduled our dinner. Everything all right?"

"Everything is fine. It's just been a little crazy. Next week is still good?"

"Yes, it's fine. Have you decided to join me for this year's party?"

"I have."

"Good. You've made me a very happy man. Plan a shopping trip. I'll send the car."

"Father, that's not necessary."

"I insist."

"Then I'll let you know the date and time at dinner next week."

"Fine. I'll see you soon. Take care of yourself."

"I will. You do the same." Mercy ended the call and let out a long breath, her heart racing. She'd answered in the nick of time. She turned to Noah, who had the advantage of watching her, when it was she who wanted the privilege of studying him. She'd missed the sight of him, but this wasn't the Noah she'd memorized. The man in her dreams. This man was a stranger, but he had Noah's voice, those eyes that took her in and made her feel like the only person on earth … he'd returned.

He came to her, his strides eating up the distance between them.

"I can't believe you're here." She almost reached out to hug him but held herself in check.

"Mercy, I have to know … you asked me to stay once, but now I'm asking if you'll take me back."

Her heart yearned to leap, but hadn't it done just that so long ago when Brad had declared he wanted a future with her, only for her to find out his future was already planned with another? Then he'd had the nerve to ask her to take him back. "For how long this time? A month? Two? Until your next trip to Tennessee?"

"I want to stay as long as you'll have me. You were in my thoughts constantly, and I knew I had to come back. You made me realize hope wasn't a lie. It's in you. It's who you are."

"Because of Christ."

"I know."

The time they were away from each other had seemed so long, but as they stood only a step apart, taking each other in, the time and distance vanished between them. "If you want to stay, I have a room."

"Mercy," he whispered her name. He reached out to take her hand and gently caressed her knuckles. "Do you want me here?"

A faint "yes" escaped her lips. Her admission, his nearness, and the warmth of his touch drew her the last step to him. "I want this, but there's so little I know about you."

He searched her eyes and moved several strands of hair from her cheek, grazing her skin in the process. "I'll tell you anything."

"I was hurt once. I need more time."

"Brad?"

Mercy looked away and nodded. "He lied and hid the truth from me." She drifted a few steps back. "I know it's late. I think we should get going." She checked her pockets for the keys and her cell phone.

As they walked back to The Lighthouse, Noah strolled alongside her. She peeked at him from time to time, still taken by the fact he was here.

The motion sensor flooded the area with light. She paused near the house's front stoop while Noah grabbed his bag. "If your eye isn't better in the morning—"

"I'll be fine."

"If you change your mind, I can call Susan." She unlocked the door, and he held it for her to enter.

"Don't worry about me. Physical pain is nothing compared to losing someone. I'm glad you weren't alone tonight. Nothing else matters to me but your safety."

For Noah, a man who'd lost so much, his words carried a great deal of truth, but to Mercy, her safety was the least of her concerns. Her heart was another matter altogether.

As they walked down the hall, it suddenly occurred to her that Noah's room was taken. "There's someone in the room you were using. You'll take my old room. I need to get the key from the office."

"The attic is finished? Do you like it?"

"Oh, it's perfect." She withdrew the key from her desk and handed it to him. "They had to raise the roof. You'll have to see it."

"I'd like that."

"Tomorrow?" Her dreams of them in the apartment sharing their first kiss came to mind. Heat crept up her neck. She reached into her pocket for her phone to hide her face, anything to avoid his gaze. She read the time.

"Tomorrow. We have a lot to talk about." Noah took her palm and pressed her wrist gently against his mouth, kissing her ever so softly. "Good night, Mercy." He released her hand and strolled away.

Left breathless, she stood in her office, stunned. It took several minutes for her mind to catch up with her heart. *What did he mean by "we have a lot to talk about"?*

Slipping into bed an hour later, Mercy prayed for each resident, for every volunteer, and as her eyes grew heavy, she prayed for her heart, for the Lord to protect it. That the man she'd fallen in love with would stay this time.

CHAPTER 12

*L*ast night, Noah was at peace, felt it the moment he saw Mercy's worried face after she pepper-sprayed him. He belonged here with her, and for the first time since he'd left, he slept soundly.

But today was a different story. He was pacing Mercy's old room, now his, where he'd stayed. Breakfast would be served within minutes, and he'd see the woman he kissed. Granted, it was a kiss on the wrist, but still, it meant everything. To him. Had it meant anything to her? "Lord, so maybe I rushed things. She said she needed more time."

Time. He paused his steps. *How much time?* Life was too short. If anyone was aware of that fact, it was him.

She might not even feel the same about him, but oh, how freeing it was to feel alive again. To know God was making a way and directing him back to Mercy, back to the people she poured her heart into day after day.

Noah left the room, unsettled about what to do next. When he reached the kitchen, he found Mercy serving.

Her hair was neatly pulled back in a ponytail, and if he wasn't mistaken, she was wearing mascara. She'd never worn any type of makeup except on the days she met her father for lunch. To Noah, what first attracted him to her was the size of her heart, her ability to love in a way that not many were able to, but now he enjoyed viewing God's beautiful creation. A woman he hoped would accept him as she accepted others, but also love him in return.

"Hi, Demetris." He grabbed a foam tray, then slid to where Mercy stood scooping eggs. "Can we talk when you're finished?"

"Wait. Do I know you?" Demetris asked, coming to them.

Mercy grinned. "Demetris, may I introduce you to the new Noah Allen, all the way from Tennessee."

His eyes grew wide. "No joke. Well, look at you." Laughing, he thrust out his hand for a hearty shake. "You clean up nice, man. But what happened to your eye? Face? Did you forget to turn over in the tanning bed?"

Noah gave a sly grin. "Let's just say I had a run-in with my future, and she left a mark."

Demetris' mouth curved. "Are you here to stay?"

Noah glanced to Mercy. "I hope so."

Her cheeks blushed. "Remember, I'm helping Demetris with lunch at the soup kitchen? We'll talk afterward."

"Yes, boss." Grinning, Demetris took the spoon from her. "You two go talk."

"But—" Mercy began.

"Don't you worry none. Felicity and Tucker can help

out. You know Tucker has been itching to be in that kitchen." He winked at Noah.

Noah was sure Tucker was interested only because of Mercy. "Then let's talk now. You can show me your new place."

"Don't you want to eat?"

With his nervous stomach, he couldn't if he wanted to. "I'm really not hungry. Ready?"

She looked to Demetris, but he shooed her. "I'm going. Come on, Noah, before we get thrown out."

Noah followed Mercy up her new staircase and waited until she unlocked her door. She allowed him to enter first. He couldn't believe what he was seeing—all the additional space. "This is incredible."

"You think so?"

"Don't you?" He scanned the open living space and the five-piece gray living room set. "There's so much room."

She pointed to an area that resembled a kitchen. To the right stood a table with four chairs. "I have everything but a stove. I didn't see a need for one with my meals being prepared downstairs. But if I wanted to eat up here, I could and would still have the luxury of washing my dishes in the dishwasher." She ran a hand along the white countertops, which matched the cabinets. "I love the faint gray lines running throughout the granite."

"This is very nice. What's over there?"

"I'll show you." She went down a small hallway with three doors. "To the left is a full-size bathroom and to the right are the bedrooms."

He poked his head into the rooms and followed her

back into the living room. "They did an amazing job. I'm impressed."

"I am too." She looked behind him, then down at her hands as if trying to come up with something to say.

"Mercy, while I was gone …"

She met his gaze, expectant, waiting.

"I didn't think the Lord wanted to use me again, to reach people for Him, that with my drug abuse, I wasn't worthy enough. But I was wrong. He showed me that I'm still usable. That I can help you here. With the people you minister to."

"So you came back for a job?"

"No. Yes. That's not what I'm trying to say."

Confusion clouded her expression. "I'm sorry, but I'm not hiring."

Noah rubbed the back of his neck. "Can we sit? It's been a long time since I've put myself on the line like this, and I'm messing it up terribly."

Smiling gently, Mercy led him to the couch and they both sat. "Go on."

Noah leaned back against the cushions, then sat up. "I believe the Lord brings people together for a purpose. One of those reasons is to bring Him glory in their union. Marriage is a beautiful thing. Bella and I, we were a match made in heaven. She completed me. Where one was weak, the other was strong. I never thought Bella or our son, Peter, would leave this world so soon. Their deaths took me down a lonely spiral, but after meeting you, I began to feel peace again. You soothed my soul, Mercy. I felt my heart beat again every time you were near. I began looking forward to our next time together. I started desiring your company to the point Bella seemed to fade away. Honestly, it scared me. I didn't want to lose Bella more than I already had."

Mercy nodded slowly, as if taking his words in. She looked to her folded hands in her lap, then met his gaze. "Is that the reason you left?"

"Yes, I loved Bella with all my heart, but I realized I was falling in love with you."

Mercy reached over and covered his hand with her own. The physical connection brought him peace enough to continue. No matter how hard it was to express his thoughts and feelings, this was right between them. That truth settled in every chamber of his heart.

"I missed you while you were gone," she said. "I prayed for you. There were times the Lord would jerk me out of bed, and I'd find myself on my knees. It wasn't about me or us, but about your worth in Him."

"I was afraid I couldn't be the man you needed." He clung to her hand. "That I was useless to God. Your heart for the Lord and the people here … your life is a beacon of hope. I wasn't sure I could live up to you."

Her face fell. "Why do you say that? It's not me you should be looking toward, but the Lord. He is the author of this love I have for others, this hope. Without Him, I am useless."

"The night I told you about my accident, I wanted to share everything with you, but I didn't get a chance. I was driving that night to the house of a church member who'd called and needed immediate prayer. I didn't see the other car run the red light. When the driver tried to stop, he swerved and came into my lane. He hit me head on. It was a miracle I even survived. After several operations, I was able to return as the pastor of my church."

"I'm so sorry for everything you've gone through, but the addiction … it doesn't make you useless in God's eyes. You're an overcomer, able to reach people in a different way than I can." She looked to their clasped hands. "Also, while you were gone, I felt as if the Lord was showing me you needed this place. Now, I understand why."

"Mercy, I'm here, not as a homeless man, but as a man who has fallen in love with you and wants a future by your side, as husband and wife, and in your ministry."

She removed her hand from his, and a wrinkle cut across her forehead. Her expression bordered on shock and disbelief. He wasn't sure which one. Maybe he needed to give her time to process it all. In the quiet of the moment and with only silence as her response, he slowly rose. "I guess I should be going."

She stood a little unsteadily. "I'm not ready for you to go. Stay. Sit with me for a while. With Demetris clearing my schedule, I have nothing to do for much of the day."

"Then let's go out to one of the parks. Piedmont isn't far."

Her eyes lit with anticipation. "We can have a picnic. I've not had a picnic in years." The way she was looking at him made him feel worthy to be loved by her, because what he saw in her gaze was directed toward him. Even though she hadn't said the words, she loved him.

"I'd be honored to share a picnic with you." *Or my life.*

"Then let's raid Demetris' kitchen. Come on."

CHAPTER 13

A flutter of excitement in Mercy's middle grew as Noah jogged around to the passenger side and opened her door. It was unexpected, gentlemanly, and it made her feel beautiful. "Thank you." An uncontrollable smile lifted her mouth as she got out of the car. Noah grabbed the basket and blanket from the backseat and held out his elbow for her. She slid her arm through, relishing their closeness. It brought her father's annual party to mind.

"How about the pond?" He pointed ahead.

"I'd like that." *Should she ask him if he'd be interested in going?* "The fountain is on today. It's perfect." She helped Noah spread out their blanket and set their overflowing basket beside them. "I've not been in a while. It's beautiful here. Makes you forget you're in the city." She watched as the mist from the fountain shot into the air and decided to wait on mentioning the party.

"Do you enjoy the outdoors?" He sat closer and held

out his arm in invitation. Smiling, she leaned in, and he pulled her against his chest.

"I do, but I can tell the outdoors means a great deal to you."

"I spent most of my life studying for my doctorate or preparing for sermons or counseling couples in the church office. After everything that happened, I craved the outdoors. It helps me think. I feel closer to God outside, seeing his creation."

"I wish I could say I spent time outside, but climbing the corporate ladder, then giving it all up and making The Lighthouse my life's work has left little time for much else."

He traced his fingers gently down her forearm, to her wrist, then back again. "Why did you come outside that day I was on the patio?"

Her body relaxed even more against his chest. She found it harder to concentrate. "I'm not sure. When I peeked outside and saw you alone, I planned to just say hello but decided to rock instead. I needed you to know you weren't alone." She enjoyed another pass of his finger along her arm. "I admit, it was the first time I'd ever felt completely comfortable with someone. But it felt okay and safe to let my guard down with you. Something inside me changed that day, and then later that night when you met me at my door, I knew it was the Lord working on our hearts."

"To bring us to this moment."

"Where do we go from here?"

His caresses stopped. "If I told you where I'd like us to be in a month's time, I might scare you off."

"Then you don't have much faith in me."

"Let's go for a walk before we eat. There's a spot that looks out over the city, and I'd love to share it with you." He rose to his feet, guiding her with him. He intertwined their fingers as they walked.

"Go on. Tell me."

"I love you, Mercy, and I've come to realize life is too short. I want to marry you soon."

They reached the waterfront in view of the city, but when they stopped, Mercy met his gaze. "Promise me you'll always be honest, no matter what our future holds, and love me unconditionally."

"I promise to always be truthful, to share my heart, my worries—in happy and hard times. Promise me you'll never leave me—that I won't have to live this life alone. That your love will remain unconditional."

"I promise, Noah. Until the Lord parts us."

He cupped her cheek and kissed her softly. "Will you marry me, Mercy?"

"Yes," she said against his mouth. "I'll marry you. After you meet my father." She felt him smile before kissing her again, and she would have lingered there longer if not for children's voices drawing close.

She touched his cheek and looked into his beautiful gray eyes, drawn there by the emotion, the love he had been holding back. The same love she now gave freely, like a dam bursting at the seams. "I love you."

A smile sprang to his lips. "When do I meet your father?"

"He's hosting a party next month. Would you be my

date? I'll need to be there early, but you can meet me there. It's being held at The Estate in Buckhead."

"I'd be honored."

~

The Estate's lights shone brightly from a distance. It was magnificent against the backdrop of the darkened sky. As Noah drove up to the mansion and waited behind a Jaguar, he took in the elegance. He pictured him and Mercy saying their vows there surrounded by their closest family and friends.

A valet knocked on his window.

He glanced up and nodded, briefly peeking in his rearview mirror to see the line of cars. He hurried out and handed the boy the keys to his compact car. He was about to tell him to be careful with it, but decided the boy wouldn't find the humor in it. "Thank you," he said, and followed several couples up the brick stairs through the double doors into a crowded foyer. Jazz music bubbled out from one of the rooms beyond.

Stepping aside for others to pass, he straightened and pulled the sleeves of his tuxedo, forcing the cufflinks into their proper place. He'd spent most of the day hunting a rental. It was a tad too big. He hoped others wouldn't notice.

He continued down the large foyer looking for Mercy, glancing at a group of people standing at the open bar, then looking toward another hallway showcasing artwork. He wasn't nervous about meeting Mercy's father, though today was the day of first impressions.

More importantly, he wanted to wow the woman he loved.

"Noah."

He turned to Mercy's voice, and at seeing her wide smile, his heart picked up its beating against his chest. Her hair was down, and the soft curls hung freely over her shoulders and along the V-neck of her dark gray dress.

"Hi," he said, breathless as they drew near. He kissed her cheek. "You look stunning."

She leaned into him even more. "Thank you. It took me hours to find an A-line chiffon floor-length dress. I'm glad you like it. My favorite time, though, was at the spa, but don't tell Demetris. He dislikes frou-frou."

Demetris was the last thing on his mind at seeing Mercy in this new light. Mercy Cunningham could have any husband she wanted. She was more than stunning, wealthy behind comprehension, and had a heart made from pure gold. Yet she was here with him, thinking about her dear friend. If he asked her now where she preferred to be, he was certain she'd say at The Lighthouse.

She palmed his face. "What are you thinking? You seem miles away."

He covered her hand with his own. "How blessed I am to have you in my life, and it has nothing to do with the way you're dressed or the way your hair is done. Although I'm at a loss for words at your beauty, it's your heart and your love for others that attracted me to you. I'm standing here taking it all in and admiring the woman you are."

Tears filled her eyes, and she smiled sweetly. She pressed a soft kiss to his lips. "Thank you."

A string of guests crowded in their small space and pushed them along to where the main gathering took place. One side of the room consisted of a large stage, where a band played and mics stood. Two large screens bearing a logo he didn't recognize flanked the stage. Rows of tables held candles and bouquets of pale flowers. Round tables and a dance floor occupied the back of the room. "Your father knows how to throw a party."

"He does. And speaking of, he sees us. Would you like to meet him now?"

"Sure."

As they approached, Mr. Cunningham and another man grew silent. Mercy settled her hand on her father's arm. "Father, Mr. Goodwin, I'd like you to meet Noah Allen from Tennessee."

Noah offered both men a hand and greeted them with a smile. "What a wonderful party, sir. I'm glad Mercy invited me."

Her father eyed him a moment, then glanced at Mercy. "She failed to mention it, but we're glad to have you. Isn't that right, Jackson? A friend of Mercy's is a friend of ours." Cunningham turned his full attention to Mercy. "Did you know Jackson traveled all the way from California to be with us tonight?"

"So kind and thoughtful of you, Mr. Goodwin." Mercy left her father's side and slid her hand through the crook of Noah's arm. "I hope you enjoy the evening and have a wonderful trip home. It was nice to see you again.

Now, if you both will excuse us, I would like to show Noah the grounds. It's a lovely night for a stroll."

Noah nodded a goodbye before Mercy directed him through the crowd. "Where would you like to go?"

"There was a stairway where we first entered. Let's see where it takes us."

After retracing their steps, Mercy led him up the stairway to the second floor. She pointed to a grand piano. "Do you play?"

"Not very well. Do you?"

"It's been years, but I do love the sound of a piano."

"Then I'd gladly pound on the keys." He winked.

She chuckled. "Let's not since we're alone at the moment. I want to show you something." She maneuvered through a seating area and stopped at several large windows. "I wish it was still daylight so you could see the grounds. They're gorgeous."

He stood beside her and couldn't pick out much more than the path below. "Can you see yourself being married here?"

"Yes." She met his gaze in the reflection of the window.

He couldn't tear his eyes away. "What do you think about checking on available dates?"

"I'd like that."

Her father's reflection joined theirs. "Mercy."

They turned to Mr. Cunningham.

"Yes, Father?"

"Would you join me in welcoming our guests?"

"We'd be honored to join you." She took Noah's arm and followed her father downstairs and to the stage.

Noah waited by the steps as father and daughter stood side by side on the platform.

Cunningham was the first to speak. "Ladies and gentlemen. My daughter, Mercy, and I want to thank you for joining us this evening …" He spoke a few more minutes before Mercy stepped in front of the microphone and mentioned The Lighthouse and her ongoing work. She invited the guests to participate in the effort to change the lives of the homeless in Atlanta.

Noah was drawn to her strength and the pride in her words as she spoke. *Thank you, Lord, for bringing this woman into my life. Allow me to be a blessing to her.*

Mercy descended the stage and gave him a joyous smile. "Where to next? Take that stroll outside?"

He wanted nothing more than to stroll hand in hand, but throughout the night it seemed her father had been eying them from a distance. "I would love to, but I think I need to speak to your father."

She sought her father out, and at finding him watching them, she agreed. "I can go with you."

"No. This will be better if we're alone."

"If you're sure? He can be intimidating."

"I'll be fine. I'll find you once we're finished."

Mercy squeezed his hand and walked toward a group of women sitting at one of the tables.

Noah strolled to where her father stood speaking with a group of men about investments.

Cunningham turned to Noah. "So Mr. Allen, any stock tips for us? Any investment opportunities?"

"I'm more of a low-risk investor, but my stock portfolio has allowed me to retire at thirty-eight. But please offer any suggestions. I'd enjoy hearing your thoughts."

The men spoke a few more minutes on the subject before Cunningham excused himself and Noah to another room. He was the first to speak. "Tell me, Mr. Allen, how do you know my daughter? And what have you told her to gain her attention? Because quite frankly, you're a mystery, and I don't care for mysteries where my daughter is concerned."

Under the man's stare, Noah shifted his weight. "I met your daughter at the soup kitchen a little over a year ago."

His brow shot up, and a smirk formed on his face. "You're a charity case of hers. Well, why didn't she tell me? There was no need to be deceptive, dressing you up in a tuxedo. Hope you enjoy the party, Mr. Allen." He started for the door.

"Mr. Cunningham. May I have another minute of your time?"

He paused and gradually turned. "I can spare that."

"First, I must say, in all honesty, I was a charity case, as you so eloquently pointed out. I fell into desperate times after a forest fire ripped through my Tennessee home and took my wife and five-year-old son from me. I had no will to live and wandered the streets from state to state with no purpose. I found myself hungry and entered the soup kitchen. The visits were short, but I felt the Lord moving me to return. It was during my last visit she invited me to stay at The Lighthouse." Noah took a step forward. "Your daughter was the one who rescued me. She has brought hope back into my life. Through these last months, the Lord has opened my eyes and heart again. Your daughter is an exceptional woman, and I plan to marry her as soon as she's ready."

"Have you proposed?"

"I have."

His eyes tightened at the corners before the line of his sight fell. "And she accepted." He strolled to the window and looked out, placing his hands behind his back. "Tell me, Mr. Allen, of your education."

"I graduated with an engineering degree, but shortly afterwards, I began the long road to acquiring a PhD in Divinity."

"Did you receive your doctorate?"

"Yes, sir, but I must tell you, my plans are not to marry Mercy and sweep her away from the incredible job she's doing in your community. Her heart, her love for people, it's what drew me to her. She's right where she belongs, making her dreams come true. She is an amazing woman, Mr. Cunningham. I don't know how she fell in love with a bum off the streets, but I will stand by her side and support her ministry however she needs me to.

"Anything else?"

What did the man want to know? "I speak three languages. I have property in Tennessee but recently sold several acres to—"

"How do you plan to support yourself?"

Support myself? "I'm not sure what you're getting at. As I mentioned earlier, I'm retired. I invested wisely."

"Then you wouldn't mind signing a prenuptial agreement."

Noah stood there, mind racing to know what to say next. He never saw this coming. To imply that he'd use Mercy for her money made his stomach sour. "I'll sign whatever you want. But I'm not marrying her because of who you are. I'm marrying Mercy because of who she is —a gift I plan to cherish. Now, if you'll excuse me, sir, I'd like to get back to my date." He headed for the door.

"Noah."

He stopped but clinched his jaw to keep from saying anything.

"Keep this between us. I'll be contacting you soon."

Noah continued down the hall to find Mercy. He was ready for that stroll.

CHAPTER 14

*M*ercy knew something had happened between her father and Noah. She saw it in his demeanor, the quietness as they walked The Estate grounds. Whatever it was still seemed wedged between them three days later. He spent more time away visiting parks in the area. On occasion he'd invite her, but he spent most of his time alone. Perhaps she should just ask Noah what was said, but she thought going right to the source was her best course of action.

She grabbed her purse and found Demetris in the kitchen. "Anything else you need while I'm at the store?"

"Hamburger buns and ketchup."

"When Noah returns, please let him know I'll be back shortly."

"Will do." Demetris busied himself patting out meat.

Mercy hurried out to her car and started the engine. She didn't want anyone to know where she was off to besides the store. She backed out of the parking space and headed for her father's office. Hopefully, she hadn't missed him.

As she drove, she thought of Noah and how he'd caressed her arms as they watched a movie last night on her couch. How their kisses lingered, and how for the first time she didn't want him to leave her apartment. Though they never spoke of it, the lines of propriety were becoming blurred in her mind. She now understood his desire to marry quickly as they were together constantly under the same roof, and temptation grew daily. Perhaps it was the reason she felt he was holding himself back from loving her fully. He'd seemed to have put an inviolable space between them that kept him a true gentleman. And suddenly she knew it was the Lord.

After parking at her father's office, Mercy rode the garage elevator to the first floor before taking another elevator to the top floor. She exited, and finding his secretary wasn't at her desk, she proceeded to his office and found him nose deep in paperwork. She knocked on the open door. "I'm not surprised to see you still here."

He looked up with a smile, but it faded. He stood. "Is everything all right? You look a mess."

Mercy touched her hair. She'd forgotten to brush it. "I was in a rush to speak with you."

"It must be important. Please sit. Tell me what's on your mind."

"I think I'll just stand." She set her purse down in the chair and met his gaze. His expression was concerned, and his frown softened her heart and words. "Dad, what did you say to Noah? That night at the party, he was quiet. Wasn't himself. I thought whatever was said would pass, but yesterday a courier delivered an envelope with papers for him to sign. After signing, he became quiet again. He seems wounded by whatever was inside."

"Did you ask him about it?"

"Yes, he said you both had agreed on something, and he was holding up his side of the deal. What deal did you make with him?" As she spoke, a realization set in and grew an ache in the pit of her stomach. "Oh, Dad ..." She removed her purse from the chair, set it on the floor, and lowered to the seat. "Please tell me you didn't ask for a prenup."

"My daughter, I have your best interests in mind—"

She stood quickly, her heart pricking at the insinuation, and pressed her hand against his desk, inching forward. "Can't you trust my judgment? Noah isn't that type of man. He's honest, trustworthy. He spurs my faith as I watch him rekindle his relationship with the Lord. Since he's been in my life, he's done nothing but stand by my side and support me in my decisions. He shows me he loves me, not only by his actions but also by his words ..." The fire she felt a moment ago dwindled as the praise she spoke of Noah found its way through her mind and into her heart. "Dad, he's such a good man." She slouched back to the armchair. "Why haven't I made more of an effort to set a date?" she spoke to herself.

"I considered that question myself."

She met his gaze. "What?"

He opened a desk drawer and removed a manila envelope. "We are a lot alike, daughter. We aren't risk takers until we're sure, and sometimes we test the ones we love." He ambled over to her and handed her the envelope. "This is for you. Do as you please."

She accepted, though there was no reason to open it. She knew what it was. "I don't know what to say."

He rested against the desk in front of her. "I know you were hurt before, but you can't hold that hurt against someone else. Noah is not that man."

"I know he's not."

"Then you need to let it go. Noah loves you. The way he spoke on your behalf at the party, there's no doubt. He's an intelligent man who knows his mind."

"He wanted to marry weeks ago, but I told him he needed to meet you."

Her father held out his arms, and she went to him eagerly, dropping the envelope. "Then marry him, Mercy. You have my blessing. Love him as you've always dreamt of loving someone. Be true to yourself and to him, and hold God close to your heart."

Tears sprang to her eyes. "Thank you, Dad."

He moved her to arm's length, and she was touched by the moisture filling his eyes. "But you know you cannot be married looking like this."

She chuckled, and a smile lifted his mouth. "We've already discussed a venue, but I'm certain there isn't an open slot. Do you have any suggestions? We'd like an outside wedding. Noah loves the outdoors."

He patted her hand and strolled to the other side of his desk, fingering his calendar. "What day are you thinking?"

She bent down to look at his calendar and noticed the time on his desk. "I need to go. Everyone thinks I've gone to the store for hamburger buns and ketchup. I've not been yet." She collected the envelope and stuffed it into her bag. "I should talk with Noah first."

"Call me with the details. I'll do the best I can." He walked her to the door. "Which venue were you thinking?"

"The Estate." She gave him a quick peck on the cheek. "Love you."

When Noah returned from the bank and the jewelry store, Demetris informed him Mercy hadn't answered his many calls. At first, he wasn't concerned, though the grimace on Demetris' face said he should be. He pushed the thought aside and went to his room with the engagement ring he'd bought. But when he returned to the kitchen and Mercy still hadn't been heard from, Noah decided to head to the grocery store she frequented. However, when he returned and Mercy was still missing, he began to panic and call her repeatedly.

Now, Noah paced the outdoor patio, and each step brought on more worry. Mercy should have been back hours ago. It wasn't like her to be late to serve dinner. Demetris was holding the food warm while they waited. Noah didn't want to upset anyone so here he was.

In the rational corner of his mind, he knew he was getting ahead of himself—she was probably perfectly fine

—but the feelings of old were haunting him. The unknown, the waiting. The horrific end.

"Lord, please," he begged after each pass of the furniture. "Please, let her be okay. I won't make it through this time." The thought of losing Mercy brought him to his knees, hard against the concrete. "I'm selfish, Lord. I want a life with her."

The door opened behind him, and he turned.

Mercy stood in the doorway, looking so beautiful she might have been an angel. "Noah?"

His heart gave way to his tears, and she blurred in his vision. He shoved to his feet and in two strides had her close in his arms. Her purse fell to the floor. He trailed kisses along her jaw in search of her mouth, and at finding her tender lips, he gave in to the need of her and deepened the kiss. He praised God at the feel of the woman he loved against him, the kiss of her lips, the peace in her safety.

"I'm thankful you're all right," he breathed, kissing her hairline, his heart racing.

She held him tight, her pulse erratic against the kiss he placed on her neck. "Forgive me. I went to see my father. I lost track of time. Demetris told me you both tried to call. The ringer was off. It's on now. My phone was at the bottom of my purse. If I'd known ... I should have called."

He said nothing as his fingers found their way through her hair. He wasn't ready to let her go, but the mention of her father brought him back to reality. He rested his head against hers, taking in long breaths.

"Aren't you curious why I went to see him?"

He released her then, running a thumb along her jawline where he'd kissed. "No, Mercy. I'm not. I realize I'm not the man he wants for you."

She moved from his touch and went to her purse, its contents scattered on the ground. She lifted a manila envelope and handed it to him. "This is for you."

He eyed her as he took the envelope. Was this what he thought it was? He undid the clasp and withdrew the prenuptial agreement. The only line filled out was his signature. "I don't understand."

"I didn't either. The quietness between us, the extra time you needed away at the park, but it began at the party. I had to see him. I needed answers, and when I confronted him, he handed me this envelope."

"But my signature is the only one."

"I love my father, but he was testing you, to see if you were a man of your word. If you genuinely loved me."

"Money means nothing to me, Mercy. But if I lost you …"

She took the paper from him and tore it from top to bottom. "What is mine is yours, and what is yours is mine. We're in this together."

Noah reached into his pants pocket and withdrew a small black box. "The reason I've been spending extra time at the park lately is because I needed an excuse to slip away to get you this." He opened the box and presented Mercy with a one-carat diamond set in yellow gold.

She covered her mouth with her hand, and tears filled her eyes. "Noah, it's beautiful."

He removed the ring from the box and held it out to her. "Mercy, are you sure you want to marry me?"

"Of course. Yes. I can't wait to be your wife."

He slid the ring onto her finger and brought her hand to his lips and kissed her knuckles. "Have you set a date?"

Mercy's phone rang against the ground where it lay, and she glanced toward it. "It's my father. Do you mind?"

"No. Good ahead." Noah unwillingly released her.

Mercy lifted the phone from the concrete and answered. "Hi."

He began picking up the ripped pieces of paper that had once been a prenuptial, or had claimed to be. Had her father truly been testing him? Would he be happy for them?

"Wow, that will be perfect. Let me see what Noah thinks. I'll call you right back."

He stuffed the papers in the envelope, curious as to what caused the joy on her face. "Good news?"

She came to him, her face aglow. "The Estate, it's available for our wedding. My dad spoke with the owner, and they had a last-minute cancellation. It's in three days. Are you in?"

He stared, shocked her father was leading the way for their marriage. Of course, Noah was in, but would she regret the sudden decision? And was she truly all right with a rushed wedding and no time to prepare? "You don't have a dress."

"I don't care if I get married in a paper sack as long as we get married."

His heart began to race. "Are you sure?"

Mercy cupped his cheek and pressed a gentle kiss to his jaw. She met his gaze. "Blissfully sure."

"Then call him back." The urgency in his tone drew a smile from her.

She dialed. Mercy spoke to her father and gave him the okay to book The Estate for their wedding. A moment later Noah was kissing her, thanking the Lord for all He'd done.

CHAPTER 15

I'm getting married.

      Mercy paused in packing her suitcase. She still couldn't believe it. She'd never been so nervous and excited in all her life.

She checked her cell for the fifth time in two hours. Her father was sending two cars, one for her and one for Noah, within the hour to take them to get prepared for the wedding, then carry them to The Estate.

She heard a knock on her apartment door, certain it wasn't Noah. They'd seen each other earlier in the morning to discuss their plans for the house, as had been their routine over the last few days. Noah would soon be taking over the financial aspect while she focused on everyday operations. They'd also discussed community opportunities. He suggested leading a Bible study before the soup kitchen opened for their lunch meals, then perhaps another study with the residents at The Lighthouse. Mercy was thrilled with the upcoming changes. She couldn't wait to start her life with Noah.

"Yes," she said, opening her door to find Demetris wearing a large grin.

"Can you meet me in the kitchen for a few minutes?"

She did have almost an hour and was already packed. "Of course. I'll be down in a minute."

"Good. I'll see you there."

When Mercy entered the kitchen, Demetris was waiting with Noah at a table. "What's going on?" She looked between them.

"I have no idea. Demetris?"

Demetris went into the kitchen and returned with a peach pie. "In my family we have a tradition. On the couple's wedding day, they are presented with their first gift of a peach pie. It symbolizes a life of love, hope, and peace. I pray that God will renew your marriage daily in love and in hope for a glorious future and will fill you both with a peace that only He can provide."

"Demetris." Mercy stood and hugged his neck. "Thank you, my dear friend."

"Yes, thank you, Demetris." Noah stood and shook his hand.

Demetris sniffed. "Let me round up some plates. You both sit." When he returned with the plates, he cut into the pie and served them. "Hope you enjoy." He started to leave the kitchen.

"Demetris," Mercy called. "Where are you going? Come eat with us."

"I need to remind everyone planning to attend the wedding what time to be ready. Your father is sending transportation, and I don't want to be late. I'll see you there." He left the two to eat their pie.

Noah was the first to take a bite. "Wow, this is delicious."

Mercy took her own and moaned. "What did I tell you? He's the best."

"Are you packed for our honeymoon?" He took another bite.

"It's kinda hard when you don't know where you're going."

He moved a strand of hair from her eye and tucked it behind her ear. "We can always buy what we need when we get there."

She leaned into him for a kiss, and oh, how sweet it was.

Noah's phone chimed on the table. He checked the screen. "My car is here." He met her gaze and stood. "I'll see you soon. I love you, Mercy." He kissed the top of her head and left.

She ate a few more bites before putting the pie away and cleaning up the crumbs on the table. Her car should be arriving soon, but she enjoyed the familiar, the comfort she found here.

Making her way to her room, she thought of Noah, about when he left that final time. She'd asked him not to go, but he had, only to return to her a new man. One that desired a life with her.

Her phone chimed. She glanced down at her screen. Her car was waiting. She hurried to collect her things and found, lying next to her purse, a letter addressed to her.

She opened the envelope and withdrew the note. As she unfolded the paper, a check appeared. It was written out to Mercy Allen in the amount of $150,000.00. Noah's signature was scribbled on the bottom line. She hurried to read the letter.

Dear Mercy,

I can't begin to express how much my life has changed since I first saw you. From that moment on, I couldn't shake the thought of you. Everywhere I traveled, you were there, and the last time I left, it hurt to leave you. But here we are now, soon to be husband and wife. I can't thank the Lord enough for sending me to your doorstep and leaving me there for you to love.

You once said whatever was mine was yours, and whatever was yours was mine. Enclosed in this letter is my wedding gift to you for The Lighthouse. I know the Lord will multiply it and meet our future needs as we reach our community and city for Him.

I love you, Mercy. I can't wait to share our lives together.

With much love and affection,

Noah

EPILOGUE

here was she?
Mercy crawled on the floor in her pj's.
"Come out. Come out. Wherever you are." She heard a little squeal in the corner of the room.

Noah walked into the bedroom, and Mercy pressed a finger to her lips. "Have you lost her again?" he said, smiling. "I guess someone won't be having eggs this morning."

Emma popped to her feet. "Me woan eggs, Daddy. Peas."

Noah scooped up their daughter and kissed her cheek. "Okay. I guess you can." He looked to Mercy. "I have everything on the table, but Shameka called. I told her you'd call her back. It seemed important."

Mercy nodded and waited for Noah to close the door before calling. The phone rang once before someone answered. "Shameka?"

"Mercy, I'm callin' to let you know they's movin' me again."

"Oh, where to?" She gripped the phone tighter.

"They ain't sayin', but I had to call and let you know."

"Love you, Shameka. You'll get through this. God won't leave you. I promise."

"Thank you, Mercy. I don't know whens I'll be callin' again."

"It's okay. I'll be here or Noah will. We'll be praying for you."

"Bye, Mercy."

There was a click on the other end, and Mercy ended the call. She sat on the edge of the bed and closed her eyes. "Lord, protect Your child. Give her peace and allow her to feel Your presence. Help her to not feel alone."

Mercy thought back to the day Shameka showed up for Noah's Bible study at the soup kitchen. It surprised everyone, especially Mercy. It had been months since she'd seen her, but from that moment on, Mercy and Noah had been praying for her. Now, she was on the road to recovery and healing, though she had a long road ahead.

Noah poked his head into the room. "Are you still on?"

"They're moving her to another women's shelter, but she doesn't know where."

Noah sat alongside her and brushed a wayward hair from her face. "God has her in the palm of His hand. Trust Him."

"I know you're right."

He laid a gentle hand on her baby bump. "I think someone is hungry."

She smiled. "Is he?"

"Yes, he's a growing boy, and his momma needs to take care of herself too."

Mercy reached over and ran a hand down the scruff of his jaw. His gray eyes held her breathless. *Thank you, Lord,* she whispered in her heart. *Thank you for Your many blessings and endless mercies.*

MORE ABOUT TANYA EAVENSON

Tanya Eavenson is an award-winning Christian romance novelist. She enjoys spending time with her husband and their three children. Her favorite pastime is grabbing a cup of coffee, eating chocolate, and reading a good book. You can find her at her website, Facebook, or at her readers group, Tanya's Books & More.

CHRISTIAN ROMANCE

A New Heart

Don't miss the adventure, romance, and sometimes mystery in the next Christian and inspirational series, GEORGIA PEACHES, where each novella ends with a happily ever after in spite of a number of obstacles.

CONTEMPORARY ROMANCE

To Gain a Mommy

GAINING LOVE NOVELLA BOOK ONE

Thirteen years ago, pediatrician Hope Michaels was the fool-hearted girl who came home from college to learn the man she loved was engaged to her twin. But now to move on with her life and accept a proposal of marriage, she must confront the one man who holds the key to the wounds of her past. Fire Captain Carl McGuire can put out any flame, except for the one Hope sparks within him. As she stirs up his life and heart, Carl knows some things never change. Even a past he'd rather keep hidden. When a new neighbor moves in across the street who would be a perfect fit for their family, Mary and Brody form a plan to bring their dad and Hope together. But how will it work if Hope keeps pushing him away?

To Gain a Valentine

GAINING LOVE NOVELLA BOOK TWO

Pediatrician Patrick Reynolds works wonders with sick children, yet when it comes to pets, he's clueless. But caring for his sister's menagerie while she's on vacation is the perfect answer to working through a broken engagement. Hoping to escape the memories, he returns to his hometown, the last place he'd expect to find love. Life as a single mom is never easy, but pet shop owner Amabelle Durand has found contentment. When an old friend returns to care for his sister's pets, he enlists her assistance to keep the animals alive. But when Amabelle's young daughter falls ill, she finds herself attracted to more than the handsome pediatrician's medical skills. As Valentine's Day approaches, will Patrick and Amabelle miss out on the love they've always desired? Or will their love take flight under the stars on this very special night?

To Gain a Bodyguard

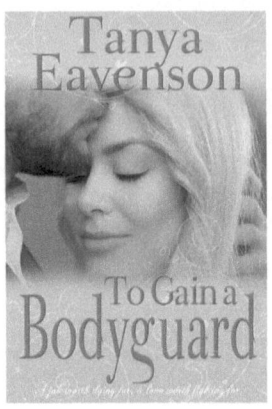

GAINING LOVE NOVELLA BOOK THREE

Undercover agent Madi Reynolds has spent years infiltrating a human-trafficking ring, but when her life is threatened, she is advised to leave the country with her bodyguard. War Veteran and ICE agent Brice Johnson has been defending his country and American lives for as long as he can remember. Now, he faces the biggest assignment of his life—protect the woman he loves. He's never been one to run from a fight, but when crippling visions of war call out to him, he begins to wonder if surrender is an option after all.

To Gain Forever

Gaining Love Novella Book Four

Karianne Bennett, small-town wedding coordinator, has always
believed in happily-ever-afters. That is, for everyone but
herself. But then hope comes when she adopts a retired service
dog and a cat-walking newcomer catches her eye. Trey Scott
has been fascinated with fireworks since he was a boy. If he can
land the festival account in an out-of-state town, he'll be that
much closer to achieving his lifelong goal. His dreams never
included a beautiful dog walker who also happens to be the
stranger he's been praying over for years.

UNENDING LOVE SERIES BOOK ONE

Elizabeth Roberts can't remember her past, and the present is too painful. She turns to nightclubs and drinking to forget her infant daughter's death, her husband's affair. When his wife's coma wiped out the memory of their marriage, Chris Roberts found comfort elsewhere. He can't erase his betrayal, but with God's help he's determined to fight for Elizabeth at any cost. She wants to forget. He wants to save his marriage. Can they trust God with their future and find a love that's unconditional?

Unending Love Series Book Two

Dr. Steven Moore is known nationally for saving lives. If only he could save his own. Unable to deal with his prognosis, he retreats to a happier time in his past—to the woman who once stole his heart. Four years after the death of her beloved husband, bookstore owner Elizabeth Roberts still struggles to sustain her faith and joy in the Lord as she raises her two sons. She strives to find a way through her family's grief, never suspecting a man from her past might offer hope for her future. But how can there be a future when he's only come to kiss her and says good-bye?

HISTORICAL ROMANCE

The Rescue

ALL ROADS LEAD TO TEXAS SERIES BOOK ONE

Rosalind Standford's life shatters when she is forced into a betrothal to a cunning banker. But when a telegram arrives announcing the man who captured her heart is on a train to Boston, Rosalind must hide her true feelings before the thin cord of her existence unravels the deadly secrets she keeps. Cowboy Trent Easton returns to his roots in Boston society to find his childhood friend, now a broken woman, engaged to a man close to her father's age. Though she once rejected him, when Trent learns she's in danger, he determines to do whatever it takes to keep her safe—even taking her to the altar in the black of night. But will his name and the remote wilds of his Texas ranch be enough to protect her? Or will freedom cost them their lives?

The Proposal

All Roads Lead to Texas Series Book Two

Coming Winter 2020

Jessica Thomson is fleeing the man who killed her father. But her stagecoach is robbed, and when the stranger who rescues her declares she will be his wife, she does the only thing she knows to do—shove her revolver in his back. Never would she have expected he wore a star on his chest. Too bad she vowed never to love another lawman. As sheriff, Blake McKenny prides himself on protecting his town's people from danger, but his efforts didn't include a headstrong woman bent on putting herself in harm's way. When outlaws threaten his town and put Jessica's life in danger, Blake's failure to save his late wife haunts him. Can Jessica and Blake forgive themselves for the past and protect each other—even if that costs them their hearts in the process?